"Your kisses say somethin' totally different, darlin'."

"It was one kiss—and it never should have happened."

"My mama might have raised me to be a gentleman," Corey said, "but she also taught me to never back down from a challenge."

"That wasn't a challenge," she said.

"Wasn't it?"

"No," she insisted vehemently, desperately. "It was a statement of fact."

He smiled again. "We'll see about that, darlin'."

"And stop calling me darlin'."

"My apologies…Erin."

The way he spoke her name made it sound more intimate than any words of passion that had ever been whispered between lovers in the dark. She fought the urge to shiver. She refused to give any outward indication of the effect of his nearness on her.

Dear Reader,

Long before I ever wrote my first book, I was a reader—and especially a reader of romance novels. From Victoria Alexander to J. R. Ward and all the authors and genres in between, I love nothing more than to lose myself in a good love story. And a good love story with a cowboy hero is especially irresistible to me, so I was thrilled to be part of the Montana Mavericks: Thunder Canyon Cowboys continuity.

Maybe Corey Traub isn't a full-time cowboy, but he has the attitude and the swagger and more than enough sex appeal to set Erin Castro's heart pounding. But she came to Thunder Canyon looking for answers, and the last thing she needs is a romance with a "too sexy for his own good" cowboy—even if that turns out to be exactly what she wants....

I hope you enjoy Corey and Erin's story and that you have as much fun visiting Thunder Canyon as I did.

Happy reading,

Brenda Harlen

THUNDER CANYON HOMECOMING

BRENDA HARLEN

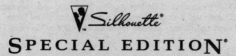

SPECIAL EDITION®

Published by Silhouette Books

America's Publisher of Contemporary Romance

Special thanks and acknowledgment to Brenda Harlen
for her contribution to
Montana Mavericks: Thunder Canyon Cowboys.

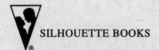 SILHOUETTE BOOKS

ISBN-13: 978-0-373-65561-8

Recycling programs
for this product may
not exist in your area.

THUNDER CANYON HOMECOMING

Visit Silhouette Books at www.eHarlequin.com

Printed in U.S.A.

Books by Brenda Harlen

Silhouette Special Edition

Once and Again #1714
*_Her Best-Kept Secret_ #1756
The Marriage Solution #1811
†*One Man's Family* #1827
The New Girl in Town #1859
***The Prince's Royal Dilemma* #1898
***The Prince's Cowgirl Bride* #1920
††*Family in Progress* #1928
***The Prince's Holiday Baby* #1942
‡*The Texas Tycoon's*
    Christmas Baby #2016
‡‡*The Engagement Project* #2021
‡‡*The Pregnancy Plan* #2038
‡‡*The Baby Surprise* #2056
§*Thunder Canyon Homecoming* #2079

Silhouette Romantic Suspense

McIver's Mission #1224
Some Kind of Hero #1246
Extreme Measures #1282
Bulletproof Hearts #1313
Dangerous Passions #1394

*Family Business
†Logan's Legacy Revisited
**Reigning Men
††Back in Business
‡The Foleys and the McCords
‡‡Brides & Babies
§Montana Mavericks:
    Thunder Canyon Cowboys

BRENDA HARLEN

grew up in a small town surrounded by books and imaginary friends. Although she always dreamed of being a writer, she chose to follow a more traditional career path first. After two years of practicing as an attorney (including an appearance in front of the Supreme Court of Canada), she gave up her "real" job to be a mom and to try her hand at writing books. Three years, five manuscripts and another baby later, she sold her first book—an RWA Golden Heart winner—to Silhouette Books.

Brenda lives in southern Ontario with her real-life husband/ hero, two heroes-in-training and two neurotic dogs. She is still surrounded by books (too many books, according to her children) and imaginary friends, but she also enjoys communicating with "real" people. Readers can contact Brenda by email at brendaharlen@yahoo.com or by snail mail c/o Silhouette Books, 233 Broadway, Suite 1001, New York, NY 10279.

For two of my most loyal readers:

Marjorie Gennings,
a wonderful aunt who has been there for me
through every stage in my life;

and

Marilyn Bellfontaine,
a true friend who has supported my career
not only from the beginning but
'above and beyond.'

And with sincere appreciation
to the other authors in this series for sharing histories,
brainstorming details, answering last-minute questions,
and making this project such an enjoyable one.

Chapter One

Erin Castro stood at the front of the church and tried not to fidget.

It was Erika and Dillon's wedding day and she knew that the attention of all of the guests was focused on the bride and groom, but since she'd arrived in Thunder Canyon, she'd worked hard to blend in and couldn't help but feel uncomfortable with so many eyes turned in her direction.

Her fidgeting fingers found the wide ribbon that bound her bouquet. The satin was smooth and cool, and the rhythmic winding and unwinding of it gave her something to concentrate on rather than the crowd of onlookers.

When she'd come to town a few months earlier, she'd had two suitcases in the trunk of her secondhand Kia, a newspaper clipping in the pocket of her faded jeans and absolutely no clue how to begin the quest she had set herself upon. Then she'd seen the "Help Wanted" sign in the front window of The Hitching Post and had taken the first step in her journey.

She'd worked with Haley Anderson at the restaurant and when Erin mentioned that she didn't want to live at the Big Sky Motel forever, Haley had helped her find an apartment. With both her job and housing concerns alleviated, Erin had believed that she was meant to stay. A few weeks later, she learned of a position available at the Thunder Canyon Resort. Realizing that the more people she encountered, the more likely she was to find someone who might have answers to the questions that prompted her trip from San Diego, Erin willingly took on the second job. When she started working a lot of overtime at the resort, she'd had to give up the waitressing job, but she had no regrets. It was at the resort that she'd met Erika Rodriguez, who was now exchanging vows with Dillon Traub.

She was happy that her friend was marrying the man of her dreams, but she couldn't help wishing that she was watching the nuptials from somewhere in the back of the church rather than the front. She wound the ribbon around her finger again as her eyes moved restlessly over the assembled crowd, focusing more on the stunning white décor of the winter wonderland setting than on any of the guests.

Her thoughts and her gaze continued to wander, until caught by the hot, intense stare of Corey Traub—the groom's brother.

Her breath stalled, and her heart pounded.

She'd met Corey the night before at the rehearsal. And her response to his presence had been just as powerful then as now—and just as unwelcome.

Her reasons for coming to Thunder Canyon hadn't included any thoughts of romantic entanglements. Especially not so closely on the heels of the end of another relationship.

She knew that her mother had harbored great expectations for the future of her almost-twenty-six-year-old (read "virtually unmarriageable") daughter and the man she'd already envisioned as the perfect (read "willing to marry her daughter") son-in-law. And while it shouldn't have been so difficult to end a relationship that meant more to Betty than it did to her, it had been tough. More so than she'd expected. She'd always felt as if she hovered on the periphery of her family. She couldn't have said why she felt that way—it wasn't anything specific anyone had said or done, it was just a sense that she didn't quite belong, and she desperately wanted to belong. And perhaps on some level, she'd thought—hoped—that a good marriage would give her the gold star she'd longed for.

As the youngest child and the only daughter, her parents didn't have the same expectations of her that they had of their sons. One of the few things they expected was that she would meet a nice man and start a family. After only a few weeks of dating, Trevor had told her that he wanted to get married.

He'd laughed at the shocked expression on her face, then explained that he wasn't actually proposing to her. He was just putting it out there, he said, so she understood what he was looking for and so that she could let him know if she didn't want the same thing.

She *wanted* to want the same thing. She tried to make herself feel more for him than she did because she knew that her parents would approve of Trevor and she really wanted to be approved of. But in the end, she couldn't stay with a man whose kisses left her unmoved. She couldn't plan a future with a man whose touch made her want to pull away rather than press closer. She knew that physical attraction was only one aspect of a relationship, but she couldn't imagine building a long-term relationship with a man without ever feeling that little quiver in the pit of her belly.

As she looked into Corey Traub's espresso-colored eyes, she felt that quiver—and a whole lot more. There was a crackle and sizzle in the air that assured her his kisses would not leave her unmoved.

When his gaze drifted to her mouth and his own lips curved, she knew that his thoughts were following a similar path to her own. Her body's response was strong and swift, and she was shocked by the purely visceral reaction.

She wasn't the type of woman who got swept away by passion. She wasn't sure she even believed in the kind of all-consuming passion that could sweep a woman away. She'd certainly never experienced anything like it before. And what was wrong with her that she was having such thoughts about a man she barely knew—and during her friend's wedding, no less?

She resisted the urge to lift the bouquet of flowers to her face and use it as a fan to cool the heat that had suddenly infused her cheeks.

"…I now pronounce you husband and wife."

The minister's voice broke through Erin's reverie and refocused her attention.

"You may kiss your bride," he told the groom.

She watched Dillon as he lowered his head toward Erika's, and the obvious love and happiness in his eyes brought tears to Erin's. Standing behind Erika, she couldn't see the expression on her friend's face, but she knew Erika's eyes would reflect the same emotion and joy. Erika had been floating on cloud nine since she'd finally accepted that Dillon loved her and admitted that she felt the same way about him. This wedding was just the icing on the cake—a public ceremony to affirm the love they shared and formalize the commitment they'd already made to one another.

Erin was surprised to realize that she envied her friend. Surprised to realize that getting married and starting a family might not be as far down on her list of priorities as she'd suspected. Of course, she'd have to fall in love first, and she wasn't looking for any kind of personal involvement right now.

She'd never been all the way in love before. Sure, she'd experienced attraction and infatuation and there had even been a time or two when she'd thought what she was feeling might be love. But when those relationships had ended and she'd felt more relief than regret, she'd known it wasn't. And the relief had given way to doubt as she wondered if she would ever know the intensity of emotion that was supposed to be love.

Her parents had it—she recognized it in the looks that passed between them, the casual touches they exchanged, the secret smiles they shared. Even after more than thirty years of marriage, there was an enduring bond of both attraction and affection between them that Erin someday hoped to find with someone.

Of course, her life was too unsettled right now to be making any kind of long-term plans, but…someday.

She glanced at Corey again and found his eyes still on her. Her future might be uncertain, but she wasn't immune to the attraction of a handsome man.

And she found herself wondering what it would be like to be held by him, kissed by him. She wanted him to take her in his arms and hold her tight against his hard body until she was breathless. Which would take all of about half a second considering that just the *thought* of kissing him stole all the air from her lungs.

She tore her gaze from his and forced the treacherously enticing thoughts from her mind.

Because she had no doubt that the six-foot-tall oil heir

had kissed more than his fair share of women and she had no intention of joining the undoubtedly long line of willing women he had left behind. And he would be leaving—he might have family in Thunder Canyon, but his home was in Texas and her home was…well, she hadn't quite figured that out yet.

Which was just one more reason that any kind of involvement with Corey Traub would be both foolish and reckless.

When the bride and groom's kiss finally ended, even the minister was smiling his approval. Then he turned to the assembly and said, "Ladies and gentlemen, it is my pleasure to introduce to you Dr. and Mrs. Dillon Traub."

The guests all rose to their feet and applauded.

Dillon took Erika's hand with one of his and held out the other to Emilia, his two-year-old stepdaughter. The little girl's bright, happy smile made Erin smile, too. Her friend had harbored doubts about Dillon's willingness to be a father to someone else's child, but the sexy doctor had proved that he wasn't just ready to step up but was eager to do so, and it was obvious to everyone present that the bride and groom and tiny flower girl were already a family.

Erin felt an ache in her heart as she thought of her own family and the questions that had brought her to Thunder Canyon. Questions that remained, after more than three months in town, unanswered.

Her parents still didn't understand what had precipitated her sudden decision to pack up and head to Montana. She'd claimed dissatisfaction with her job and the relationship with Trevor, but she knew they were worried, that they felt she should have tried to change the situation rather than run away from it. But after her last meeting with Aunt Erma, only hours before the elderly woman passed away, she'd realized that she needed answers her parents couldn't—or wouldn't—give her. Answers that might finally explain why she'd always felt a little out of place in her own family.

You need to find your family. Her aunt's words echoed in her mind. *They're in Thunder Canyon.*

Erin had been as stunned as she was skeptical, especially when Erma didn't provide any more information. As for the newspaper clipping the elderly woman had given to her, Erin still didn't know what to make of that. She didn't have a clue which of the families in the photo—if any—might be able to help her find the answers she sought, and Erma hadn't steered her in a specific direction.

She hadn't shown the clipping to her parents—a decision that she continued to wrestle with. But both Jack and Betty had been dismissive of Erma's claims. When Erin had asked if she'd been adopted, her mother had offered to show off the stretch marks and unsightly veins that were her reward for the nine months that she'd carried her daughter.

But there was something about Erma's words that haunted Erin in a way she didn't understand and couldn't disregard.

If she wasn't adopted, maybe her parents had gone through a rough patch in their marriage and her mother had been involved with someone else. It had taken a lot more courage to ask Betty about *that* possibility, but her mother had actually laughed, assuring Erin that there had never been anyone before her father and never anyone since.

Still, she couldn't help but feel that there had to be some kind of foundation for Erma's conviction. Unfortunately, her aunt's death had left Erin with a lot of doubts and uncertainties, countered only by her determination to find the truth once and for all.

"Shall we?"

The question jolted her out of her reverie and made her realize that the bride and groom had already started down the aisle. She forgot about Erma and all of her reasons for coming to Thunder Canyon when she settled her hand in the crook of Corey's elbow.

She concentrated on putting one foot in front of the other as she followed Dillon and Erika and Emilia, refusing to look at the groom's brother. But as they approached the doorway, Corey pulled her a little closer to negotiate the narrow opening, and she shivered.

Thankfully, the cool November afternoon gave her a ready excuse for the goose bumps on her flesh, even if she knew they were more a response to the man at her side than the chilly weather. But she had no intention of being distracted from her fact-finding mission by anything or anyone—not even the groom's far-too-sexy brother.

It was torture, riding beside him in the limousine on the way to the resort for the reception. Although there were only five of them in a ten-passenger limo—and one of those five a child buckled into a car seat—the interior of the vehicle felt small to Erin. Or maybe it was that Corey was so big.

She shifted on the seat so that she was pressed against the side of the car. But she could still feel the heat of his body and smell a hint of his aftershave, and she couldn't help but watch the smooth, efficient movements of his hands as they peeled the foil off of a chilled bottle of champagne.

He unfastened the wire and popped the cork while Dillon struggled to unwrap the straw on a juice box for his new daughter. Erika reached for the drink, obviously trying to help, but her groom was determined to master the task. The bride shrugged and settled back against the cushy leather seat, content to let him.

Erin felt a little tug of envy again but pushed it aside. Maybe Erika did have it all, but getting it hadn't been easy for her. She'd had her heart broken when Emilia's father walked out on her, and then she'd had to tackle the trials and tribulations of single parenthood. From Erin's perspective, her friend had done a wonderful job, and if she'd lucked out when she'd fallen in love with Dillon Traub, well, no one deserved it more.

Corey had finished pouring the champagne and passed the crystal flutes around to the adults.

"To the bride and groom," he said, lifting his glass.

Erin joined in the toast but only took the tiniest sip. Although she was sure the bubbly wouldn't be nearly as potent as Corey's proximity, she didn't want to take the chance of alcohol further compromising her judgment.

"To Erika," Dillon said. "Not only the most beautiful bride I've ever seen and the most amazing woman I've ever known, but also the one who has given me the greatest gift I could ever hope for by becoming my wife today."

Erika's eyes were misty with tears when her new husband brushed his lips against hers.

"To my daughter," the groom said, tapping his glass against Emilia's juice box. "One of those greatest gifts."

The little girl beamed at him and slurped down more juice.

"And to my brother," Dillon continued. "For always being there for me when it mattered, and especially today because it mattered most of all."

Corey grinned. "I'll remind you of those words the next time you grumble about me being underfoot."

His brother smiled back before he shifted his attention. "And to Erin—"

"Wait," Erika interrupted.

Dillon's brows rose.

"As the bride, I should get to toast my maid of honor," she said.

Her husband gestured for her to continue.

Erin's fingers tightened around the stem of her glass as she felt the attention focus on her.

"To Erin. I know you were surprised when I asked you to stand up with me at my wedding, and more than a little reluctant, and I want to thank you for saying 'yes' because although we've only known each other for a few months, I feel closer to you than all of the people that I grew up with here in Thunder Canyon. More, I feel accepted by you and appreciated for who I am rather than judged by what I've done, and I will always be grateful for your unwavering support and your unconditional friendship."

"Hey, can you say something about me?" Corey asked his new sister-in-law. "Because that was a lot more eloquent than what Dillon came up with."

Everyone was laughing as the limo pulled up in front of the resort.

Erin slipped away from Corey's side soon after they entered the ballroom.

The bride and groom had opted for a champagne reception rather than a formal meal, so there was no seating plan and guests mingled freely while waiters circulated with trays of hot and cold hors d'oeuvres. Erin decided it was wise to do her mingling as far away as possible from the best man.

It was a strategic retreat. She simply didn't know how to deal with the feelings that stirred inside of her when she was near Corey. During the brief time that she'd dated Trevor, she'd been aware that something was missing. She'd liked him well enough and they'd shared some common interests, but there was no spark between them.

When Corey Traub had walked into the rehearsal the night before, she could hardly see for the sparks. She'd always thought she should feel *more,* but she had never guessed how much more there could be—or how unsettled the more could make her feel.

She had no experience with this kind of immediate and intense attraction. But she was certain that Corey did. That he had this effect on women all of the time and no doubt knew exactly how to handle it. How to handle *her*. And as intrigued as she was by the idea of being handled by the sexy groomsman, she was even more wary.

She didn't do a lot of mingling, but she made a point of chatting with the people she knew and spent several minutes talking with Haley Anderson and Marlon Cates, Haley's now-fiancé. When she turned away from the couple, she found herself face-to-face with Corey.

Actually, it was more face-to-chest because, even in heels, she was several inches shorter than he. And it was quite a chest, the breadth and strength of it evident even through the shirt and jacket he wore. She forced her gaze to lift to an even more impressive face.

Was it any wonder the man took her breath away? He had a look that could sell…anything, she decided, and managed to hold back a sigh.

He had a strong forehead, sharp cheekbones, a slightly square jaw. His brows arched over dark eyes surrounded by thick lashes, his lusciously curved mouth was quick to smile, and when he did, her knees simply went weak. The slight bump in his nose was the only imperfection, but it didn't detract from the overall effect.

But he was somehow more than the sum of all of those parts, and the devilish charm that sparkled in his eyes and winked in his smile was just one more weapon in his over-stocked arsenal.

"You've been avoiding me," Corey said, sounding more curious than offended.

"I have not," she denied, though not very convincingly.

"Prove it," he challenged.

She eyed him warily over the top of her glass. "How?"

"Dance with me."

Erin took another tiny sip of her champagne as she considered how to respond. She knew she should refuse, that getting closer to the groom's brother was not a good idea when he could make the nerves in her belly quiver from clear across the room. But how could she refuse? What excuse could she give for declining a seemingly innocent request? Especially when he'd already guessed that she was avoiding him.

Thankfully, before she could say anything, another woman approached from the other side and latched on to him, deliberately rubbing the curve of her breast against his arm as she leaned close. "Hey, cowboy, you promised me a dance."

When she'd been waitressing at the Hitching Post, Erin had gotten to know Trina as one of the Friday night regulars. Trina frequently came in with a group of girlfriends and often left with a man—and not usually the same one as the week before.

At the resort, Erin frequently worked at check-in with Trina, as had Erika. No doubt it was their working relationship that had compelled the bride to invite the other woman to her wedding despite the fact that Trina had been instrumental in churning the gossip mill when Erika started dating Dillon.

Erin didn't know whether Trina had attended the event with a date, although she knew the presence of an escort wouldn't inhibit Trina from flirting with anyone else who caught her eye—as the groom's brother had obviously done.

To his credit, Corey didn't roll his eyes, though Erin

didn't miss the quick desperate plea in them before he shifted his gaze from her to the other woman.

"But I already promised this particular dance to Erin, didn't I, darlin'?"

She had the power to save him. She simply had to agree that he had promised this dance to her. But she sensed that saving Corey from the she-wolf at his side would somehow end up with her becoming a sacrificial lamb, and that was a risk she wasn't willing to take. Because the way he said "darlin'"—the subtle Texas twang in his voice combined with the unmistakable heat in his eyes—sent a delicious shiver over her skin and stirred desire in her body and reminded her that what she needed to do was keep a good, safe distance between herself and the far-too-sexy Texas oil heir.

"Actually, I really wouldn't mind sitting this one out," she said.

"I'll be right back," Corey said to her, and his narrowed gaze told her that the words were more a threat than a promise.

Trina's satisfied smile, however, warned Erin not to count on his prompt return.

She watched him move around the dance floor with the other woman in his arms and tried to convince herself that the sensation overtaking her was relief and not regret.

Corey knew when he was being brushed off. Though it was something of a new experience for him, he had no trouble interpreting the message in Erin's polite words—she wasn't interested.

The woman in his arms, however, definitely was. Unfortunately, Corey couldn't even remember her name.

Catrina? Tina? Trina! At least, he thought that was it. He admittedly hadn't been paying much attention when she'd introduced herself earlier. He hadn't paid much attention to any of their conversation, having been thoroughly captivated by the sexy bridesmaid in the frosty blue gown.

The one who claimed she wasn't interested.

His gaze drifted across the room to where Erin stood with a glass of champagne in her hand, and his gaze locked with hers again.

And he knew that, although she might feign disinterest, the look in her eyes contradicted her words.

So what was the story there? Why was she pretending to be immune to the chemistry between them?

After meeting her at the rehearsal the night before, he'd made some discreet inquiries and learned that she didn't have a steady boyfriend. In fact, by all accounts, she hadn't dated anyone since moving to Thunder Canyon a few months earlier. Which made him wonder if she'd made the move because she needed to get away from someone who had broken her heart.

The thought was strangely unsettling. He didn't even know her, so he didn't understand why he would feel protective of her. But there was something that had struck him from the first—maybe it was the hint of vulnerability in those deep-blue eyes, or the wistfulness in her smile, or maybe it was just the feeling, irrational though he knew it was, that Erin was the woman he'd been waiting for.

He smiled at the thought, recognizing it as not just irrational but ridiculous in light of the fact that he couldn't even get her to agree to dance with him. Then again, Corey had never been one to back down from a challenge.

More and more couples were joining those already on the dance floor and soon the space was so crowded with bodies that he lost sight of her. When the song finally ended and he released Trina, she pouted prettily.

"Are you really going to let me go so soon?"

"Yes, I am, darlin'," he told her, but softened the rejection with a smile.

She tucked something into his pocket. "My number—in case you change your mind."

Because his mother had raised him to be a gentleman, he didn't tell her that he'd had her number from the start, but he also didn't give her another thought as he walked away.

He was too busy searching the crowd for a certain blue-eyed girl in a familiar blue dress.

Chapter Two

Erin had let down her guard. It was the only excuse she had for being caught so unaware. But when Corey had followed Trina onto the dance floor, Erin had been certain her coworker would keep him thoroughly occupied. She hadn't expected that he would walk away from an obviously willing woman and come looking for her.

But she'd barely started to nibble on the hors d'oeuvres she'd put on her plate when he lowered himself into the empty chair beside her. She popped a coconut shrimp in her mouth, slowly chewing then swallowing.

"I believe you owe me a dance," he said, choosing a stuffed mushroom from her plate.

She lifted a brow. "Do I?"

"At the very least."

"Why don't I share my dinner and we'll call it even?" she suggested.

He grinned, and she felt the now-familiar weakness in

her knees again. "I'll get you some more mushrooms as long as I get the dance."

She nudged her plate toward him. "I'm really not that hungry."

"What are you afraid of?" He bit into a petite quiche.

"That you'll stomp all over my toes with your cowboy boots."

She'd meant to insult him, hoped the affront would dissuade him. Instead, he laughed.

"I'm sure you'll survive," he told her. "My previous dance partner was barely limping when she walked away."

"She was plastered so close, you wouldn't have been able to step on her toes if you tried."

Too late she realized what she'd said—that her response proved that she'd watched him with Trina.

Corey's smile confirmed that he'd caught her slip, but thankfully, he didn't call her on it.

"What do you say?" he prompted.

Erin knew that to refuse again would only succeed in making a big deal out of something that shouldn't be. After all, it was just a dance.

So she took the hand he offered and let him lead her away from the table. Though her heart was hammering furiously against her ribs, she decided that there really wasn't any danger in spending time with Corey on a crowded dance floor.

The minute he put his arms around her, she realized she was wrong. Because every fiber of her being was acutely aware of his nearness and every nerve ending in her body was suddenly humming.

She should have guessed that he'd be a good dancer. Contrary to her earlier teasing remark that she feared for her feet, he moved smoothly and confidently around the dance floor. No doubt he knew all the right moves in any situation, but despite that warning to herself, it required no effort on Erin's part to follow his lead, nor was it a hardship to be held in his arms.

She saw Erika and Dillon dance by and was grateful for the distraction. "They look so perfect together," she murmured.

"I've never seen my brother so happy," Corey admitted to her. "It almost makes me forgive him for pulling up stakes and moving to Montana."

She tipped her head back. "Almost?"

He shrugged. "A Texan is always a Texan, regardless of where he parks his horse."

The mental image of a horse tethered outside of the medical clinic made her lips curve.

His gaze dropped to her mouth, lingered. Her breath caught.

"You have a beautiful smile," he told her.

Immediately, her smile faded.

"Why do I make you so nervous?"

She couldn't—wouldn't—tell him that it was her own response to him that made him nervous. Instead, she said, "Because I don't know what you want from me."

"Right now, just a dance."

"And later?"

His smile was slow and filled with sensual promise. "Why don't we figure that out later?"

"If you're looking for a good time while you're in Thunder Canyon, you should be looking in Trina's direction," she told him.

"You don't think we could have a good time together, darlin'?" The challenge was issued in that same lazy tone that skimmed over her like a caress.

"I'm sure we could," she replied honestly. "But I'm

not the type of woman to go home with a smooth-talking stranger."

He pulled her closer so that her thighs were aligned with his. They were more swaying than dancing now, and the light brushes of his body against hers felt disturbingly like foreplay.

"I'm hardly a stranger," he said.

"I just met you yesterday."

"And I haven't been able to stop thinking about you since then."

She wasn't entirely sure she could trust what he was saying. Because while he sounded sincere and the look in his eyes confirmed that he felt at least a hint of the same attraction that had her whole system tied up in knots, she couldn't help but feel that Corey Traub was the type of man who had a line for every occasion—and a woman in every town he'd ever visited. She'd be a fool to fall under his spell, and she was already halfway there.

He dipped his head toward her, his dark eyes sparkling with a hint of playfulness. "So tell me, are your toes black and blue yet?"

"You know they're not," she said.

He grinned, and again her breath caught. *Damn.* The man's smile was a seriously dangerous weapon.

"So why do you sound annoyed?" he teased.

"I'm not annoyed," she denied.

But she was wary.

Corey could see that in her eyes. And he couldn't blame her. She was probably used to being hit on by guys who wanted nothing more than to get naked with her, and although Corey wouldn't deny that idea appealed to him, he was trying not to objectify the woman who was obviously a close friend of his new sister-in-law.

Sister-in-law.

The word echoed in his mind, made him shake his head. Erin raised a brow.

"I was just thinking about the fact that I'm dancing with the most beautiful woman at my brother's wedding," he answered the unspoken query, "which made me realize that Dillon is actually married."

"Is he one of those guys who swore it would never happen?"

"I don't know if I'd say that, but he and his first wife divorced after their son died and he never gave any indication that he was looking to settle down ever again. And certainly no one expected that, when he came to Thunder Canyon to fill in for Marshall at the resort, he would fall in love and become a husband and a father only a few short months later."

"Especially not Erika," Erin noted.

He chuckled. "Yeah, I think she fought against falling in love again even more than he did."

"She had reason to be wary."

"I guess she did," he agreed. "And so did he. How about you?"

"What about me?"

"Why isn't there anyone here with you tonight?"

"I didn't see any point in bringing a date when I would only neglect him to perform my maid-of-honor duties."

Which answered his question without actually telling him whether or not she was involved with anyone right now. He decided to trust the reports of the local grapevine and assume that she was currently unattached.

But there was something else he was curious about. "You've known Erika for a while?"

"Since I moved here in the summer."

"So why were you uncomfortable in the limo when she thanked you for standing up with her?"

She lifted a shoulder. "Because I didn't really do anything that required thanks."

"You were—are—her friend."

"And she's mine."

He nodded. "But why—"

Someone nudged his shoulder.

He scowled and turned, an irritated retort on the tip of his lips until he saw that it was his cousin Dax.

"Come on, Cor. We've got bottles of champagne ready to toast the bride and groom."

"And I've got a beautiful woman in my arms," Corey pointed out to his cousin.

"I'm not suggesting you let go of her," Dax said and winked at Erin. "Bring her along."

And that was how she ended up with Corey at a table where his friends and family were gathered.

During the time she'd been in Thunder Canyon, she'd already met most of the others at the table. The Traubs—Dax and Shandie, DJ and Allaire, and the Cates—Marshall and Mia—now back from their vacation, Mitchell and Lizabeth, Marlon and Haley and Marlon's twin brother, Matt. Erin realized that Matt Cates was the only one not married or engaged, though he had brought Christine Mayhew as his date. Her boss, Grant Clifton, was also there with his wife, Stephanie, and Grant's best friend, Russ Chilton, was in attendance with his spouse, Melanie. Erin had met the rest of the groom's family at the rehearsal, but other than the parents—Claudia and Peter—she didn't remember any of their names, and she was grateful when Corey repeated the introduction of his brothers, Ethan, Jason and Jackson, and his sister, Rose.

Erin hovered on the periphery as glasses of champagne were passed around, thinking that she might be able to sneak away. But Corey kept an arm around her shoulders, making it clear that he had no intention of letting her go. So she stayed beside him as toasts were made and glasses refilled, and she found herself following the various conversations with avid curiosity.

When conversation shifted to the Thanksgiving holiday, only a few weeks away, Grant remarked that he expected his mother and his sister would both return to Thunder Canyon for the occasion.

"It's been a long time since Elise has been in town for her birthday," Grant said. "So I'm planning a surprise party for her while she's here."

"How old is she going to be?" Erin asked.

"Twenty-six," her boss replied. "On the twentieth."

Erin paused with her glass of champagne halfway to her lips.

Her twenty-sixth birthday was on the twentieth, too.

It was probably nothing more than a coincidence, but a sudden startling thought occurred to her. All this time she'd been looking for a man who might have had an affair with her mother, but maybe aunt Erma had been referring to something completely different.

Erin lowered her hand and focused her attention more intently on her boss, noticing—for the first time—that his eyes were the same blue color as her own. And that his hair was dark blond, also similar to her own. She shook her head, as if to rid it of the fanciful imaginings. But the questions that had rooted in her mind wouldn't be easily dismissed.

"I haven't seen Elise since high school," Matt remarked. "I'm not even sure if I would recognize her."

"I'm sure you would." Grant reached into his back pocket for his wallet. "She hasn't changed much."

Erin, who had been wondering how to ask Grant if he

had any pictures of his sister, leaned closer as her boss tugged a photo out from its holder and slid it across the table toward Matt.

"This was taken last summer," Grant told the other man.

Matt leaned closer to look at the photo, and Erin did, too.

"You're right," Matt said. "In fact, she hasn't changed at all."

Erin's first thought was that Grant's sister was an attractive woman—her blond hair was worn in a pageboy style that brushed her shoulders and she had pretty blue eyes and an innocence about her that made her appear younger than her years. Her second thought was that Elise didn't look much like her brother. In fact, the shape of her eyes and her chin was more like that of her own brothers, Jake and Josh.

She pulled back, her stomach suddenly churning, her heart pounding. The conversation continued around her, but she didn't hear a word of it. She couldn't think of anything but that picture of Elise.

"More champagne?"

"What?"

Corey held the bottle of champagne over her glass. Erin shook her head and set her glass on the table. "I, um, I need to get some air," she said, and slipped away from him and toward the exit.

She hadn't expected that he would follow her, but she'd only just pushed through the doors and barely registered the cold November wind on her bare shoulders before they were covered.

"You shouldn't be out here without a coat," Corey said, draping his tuxedo jacket around her.

"Now you are," she told him.

"I'm not wearing a sleeveless dress."

Her lips curved, just a little, at the thought of the all-too-masculine Texan in any kind of dress, and she slipped her arms into the sleeves of his jacket.

She could feel the heat from his body, smell the scent of his skin, and the quivering that reverberated low in her belly was almost enough to take her mind off of the kaleidoscopic thoughts swirling in her mind.

Twenty-six years earlier, on November twentieth, she'd been born in Thunder Canyon. Elise Clifton had been born on the same day in the same town. And Elise looked a lot like Erin's brothers—certainly more than she resembled Grant. Which made Erin wonder—was it possible that the hospital had somehow mixed up the two babies? Was it possible that the man she knew as her boss could be her biological brother?

"Erin?" Corey frowned and touched a hand to her cheek. "Are you okay? You look a little pale."

"Actually, I'm not feeling all that good," she told him. "I think I'd better call a cab and head home."

"I'll give you a ride, if you're sure you're ready to go."

"I am," she told him. "But you don't have to—"

"I'll take you home," he insisted.

Because he'd had a couple of beers earlier in the evening and knew he would be driving, Corey had barely touched his own glass of champagne. He didn't think Erin's had been refilled more than once, but she was obviously feeling the effects of the bubbly, and because he'd been the one who refilled her glass, he felt responsible and was determined to ensure she got home safely.

As they waited for the valet to bring his truck around, he noticed that some of the color had returned to her cheeks. Or maybe they were just pink from the cold. In either case, she didn't really look intoxicated. Her words weren't slurred and her steps weren't unsteady, but her eyes were a little glassy and, even with his jacket on, she was shivering uncontrollably.

He settled her in the passenger seat and immediately cranked up the heat. After a few minutes, her teeth stopped chattering but she kept her arms folded across her chest and continued to stare straight ahead out the window.

She was quiet during the short drive to her condo on the outside boundary of the resort property, only speaking when it was necessary to tell him to turn left or right. He kept stealing cautious glances at her, hoping for some clue as to how she was feeling, but neither her posture nor her expression gave anything away.

He'd been talking to DJ and Allaire and hadn't really paid attention to any of the other conversations. She'd been chatting with Grant and Matt, and he wondered now if either of those men had inadvertently said something that might have upset her. If so, no one else in the group seemed to have picked up on anything that might have caused her distress. Because the more Corey thought about it, the more convinced he was that Erin wasn't drunk—she was upset.

But whatever was on her mind, her silence clearly indicated that she had no intention of talking about it. Not with him, anyway.

"Right here," she said.

He pulled into a narrow driveway, behind a dark-green Kia, and turned off the engine.

"Thanks for the ride," she said, reaching for the handle before Corey could come around to help her out.

"I'll see you to your door," he told her.

"That's really not necessary."

"Necessary or not," he said, falling into step beside her,

"my mama would never forgive me if I left without making sure that you were safely inside."

"Okay, you walked me to my door," she said, stopping under the porch light. "Now your mother can hold her head up, confident she raised her boys right, and you can go."

"Not just yet," he said. "How are you feeling?"

"Fine."

She did look better, as if the effects of the champagne had already dissipated. *If* the champagne had truly been the reason for her abrupt departure.

"No nausea? No dizziness?"

She shook her head. "I'm fine," she said again. "Really. It was probably just too warm in the ballroom and once I got out into the fresh air, my head cleared."

"You're sure?"

"Yes, I'm sure." She smiled up at him, and though the smile didn't quite erase the shadows in her eyes, it made him forget his concerns and remember how much he wanted to kiss her.

"Good," he said and lowered his head to taste the sweet curve of her lips.

It was a testament to how preoccupied Erin's thoughts were that she didn't anticipate his kiss.

She'd been kissed plenty of times before, and she knew how to read the signs and signals that usually led to the first touch of lips on lips—and how to dodge that touch if she wanted to.

Not that she wanted to dodge Corey's kiss. In fact, she'd spent an inordinate amount of time wondering what it would feel like to be kissed by him. She'd wondered if the same spark and sizzle she felt when he looked at her would translate through actual physical contact...or if the anticipation of his kiss would be more exciting than the actual event.

No worries there, she thought, as his lips brushed against hers again, sending tremors of longing through her body.

He kissed the way he talked—softly and smoothly, as if he had all the time in the world. And as if he intended to spend all of that time just kissing her.

His hands skimmed up her back and, even through the fabric of the jacket she still wore, she could feel the heat of his fingertips tracing the ridges of her spine. Then his hands moved across her shoulders and down her arms.

The keys that she held slipped from her fingers and crashed to the ground.

Erin didn't even notice.

She was far too busy enjoying the slow, sensual assault on her mouth.

His tongue slid between her lips, licked lazily.

There was nothing leisurely or casual about her body's response.

Each flick and flutter of his tongue shot flame-tipped arrows of heat and hunger spearing toward her center. Every careful and unhurried pass of his hands made her blood pulse and pound.

She moved against him, and both the tempo and intensity of the kiss changed.

He drew her closer, his arms wrapped around her tighter, he kissed her deeper.

Erin felt her own arms glide up his chest, her hands sliding over impressive pecs and broad, hard shoulders to link behind his neck. He was so big, so strong, so wholly and undeniably male.

And her response was completely and helplessly female.

She shuddered and melted against him.

Corey groaned into her mouth and delved deeper.

Yeah, she'd been kissed before. But never like this. In

her experience, most men approached kissing as nothing more than a brief prelude to the main event, but not Corey Traub. His kisses were worthy of top billing. He kissed her as if she was the object of all desire and the source of all pleasure, and as if he never wanted to stop.

And Erin never wanted him to stop.

But just when Erin was about to throw all common sense and caution to the wind and drag Corey inside with her, he eased away.

"I think I should say good-night now, before I forget that my mama raised me to be a gentleman," he said.

She should have been grateful he'd backed off. She didn't know him nearly well enough to even kiss him the way she'd kissed him, never mind indulge in any of the other erotic fantasies her mind had conjured up while he'd been seducing her with his skillfully creative mouth and his dangerously talented hands.

He bent to scoop up the keys she'd dropped and put them in her hand, curling her fingers around them.

His other hand lifted to her face, his fingertips skimming lightly over the swollen curve of her bottom lip.

The gentle touch set off bursts of erotic tingles that warned her to put some distance between them before she urged him to forget his mother's teachings.

"Good night," she said softly.

He stepped back, and Erin fumbled with the keys in her hand for a moment before she found the right one for the door. She fumbled some more fitting it into the lock, but then the bolt released with a click.

Corey didn't say anything else, but he waited on the step until she'd slipped inside and locked the door again, then he turned away.

Erin watched from the window as he walked back to his car and reminded herself that she'd done the right thing, the smart thing, in letting him go. There was too much uncertainty in her life to consider any kind of personal involvement right now.

But that knowledge didn't stop her from wishing otherwise.

Chapter Three

It was a kiss, Corey reminded himself—for the umpteenth time—as he got dressed the next morning.

Yeah, it had been pretty spectacular as far as kisses go, but it was still just a kiss. Certainly there wasn't any reason for him to have lain awake into the wee hours of the morning thinking about that kiss—and the woman he'd shared it with.

But the truth was, even before they'd shared that one scorching kiss, he'd been haunted by thoughts of Erin Castro.

Thoughts of wanting to kiss Erin Castro.

He shook his head as he tugged on his jeans.

He didn't know what it was about the woman that had gotten under his skin. Sure, she was attractive in a classic blue-eyed, blond-haired, porcelain-skinned, soft curves sort of way.

Okay, more than attractive. He hadn't been giving her a

line when they were dancing and he'd told her she was the most beautiful woman at the wedding because from the first moment he'd set eyes on her, he hadn't seen anyone else.

And now that he had kissed her, now that he'd tasted the sweet seductive flavor that was hers alone, he worried that he'd made a mistake. Because now he wanted more.

Cursing himself for his weakness, he picked up his phone and dialed the number he'd obtained from directory assistance. She answered on the third ring.

"Hey, Erin, it's Corey."

"Corey?" She sounded distracted, as if he'd caught her in the middle of something. Or maybe as if she didn't recognize the name.

He was frowning over that possibility when she spoke again.

"Oh, Dillon's brother. Hi."

Dillon's brother?

That was how she thought of him? How about the man who'd taken her home the night before? The man who'd kissed her breathless and continued to kiss her until they'd both wanted a lot more?

But of course he didn't ask any of those questions. He didn't want her to confirm that he'd thought about her a lot more than she'd thought about him.

"I'm sorry I didn't make the connection right away," she said. "I just—you caught me when my mind was wandering."

"Is this a bad time?"

"No. I don't think so."

"You don't think so?" he prompted.

"Well, I guess that depends on why you're calling," she said.

"Partly just to find out how you're doing."

"I'm fine."

"You said you had too much champagne last night, so I wanted to make sure you weren't suffering any lingering effects today."

"Champagne. Right. Well, that certainly explains the… uh…"

She faltered, and he suspected that she was thinking about that kiss again. Or maybe he just wanted to believe she was thinking about it because he was.

"…the headache I had this morning," she continued. "But I took a couple of aspirin with breakfast and I'm fine now."

"Good," he said, even while silently wishing he could rid himself of the residual effects of the night so easily. But he suspected that the only thing that could cure his craving for Erin was Erin herself.

"And since you've already had breakfast—which was the other reason I was calling—why don't you let me take you to lunch?"

"Lunch?"

"You know—the meal usually served in the middle of the day," he teased.

"Yes, I do know what lunch is," she assured him. "I'm just not sure I understand why you're inviting me to have lunch with you."

"Because I don't like to eat alone. And because I really enjoyed spending time with you last night and I'd like to get to know you better."

Erin was tempted—too tempted—to jump at his invitation. And not just because she knew he would be able to distract her from the questions that had been pounding inside of her head since she'd seen that picture of Grant Clifton's sister the night before. Unfortunately, all of the reasons that Corey would be such a great distraction were the same reasons that she had to refuse. Because she was far too attracted to the man, because she couldn't think of anything else when he was near and because she could very well end up with her heart broken when he went back to Texas.

So instead of accepting, she said, "I'm afraid I may have given you the wrong impression last night."

There was a pause, as if he was surprised by her response. And he probably was because she'd no doubt given him the impression of a wild, willing woman who wanted to gobble him up in big, greedy bites.

And the impression wasn't really wrong, but it was misleading because nothing like that was going to happen between them. She couldn't let things move in that direction with him while her life was veering off course in so many other ways.

"The only impression I got," he finally said, "was that of a smart, beautiful woman who was the last thought on my mind before I fell asleep last night and the first when I woke up this morning."

"Oh. Wow." Erin didn't know what else to say. Was it the words, she wondered, that made her heart pound so fast? Or the sensual tone that turned the words into a verbal seduction?

She used her free hand to fan her flushed cheeks, grateful that he couldn't see what she was doing, couldn't know the effect that he had on her, even over a phone line.

"Then you definitely got the wrong impression because I'm really not looking to get involved with anyone right now."

"I invited you to lunch, darlin', not to shop for an engagement ring," he said.

The heat in her cheeks intensified. He was right—she was overreacting. But even an invitation to lunch was dangerous when she wasn't sure she could control her instinctive response to the man issuing the invitation.

"I know," she said. "But I still don't think lunch is a good idea."

"Because you're philosophically opposed to eating in the middle of the day?"

She had to smile. "Because you're far too charming for your own good."

"You think I'm charming?"

"I'm going to say goodbye now," she told him.

"Wait, Erin."

But she couldn't wait, because she knew that if she let him say anything else, she might very well give in—not only to his invitation but to the desire stirring again in her blood. "Goodbye, Corey."

Corey continued to hold the receiver to his ear, as if he didn't quite believe that he was hearing a dial tone instead of Erin's voice. He didn't think any woman had ever hung up on him before but, for some inexplicable reason, the realization made him smile.

As a management consultant, his professional reputation had been made on the basis of identifying a problem and determining the best solutions. He would simply analyze Erin's resistance in the same way. And if she thought he was the type of man to be dissuaded by one terminated phone call, well then, she was very soon going to learn differently.

But thinking of his business objectives made him remember that he had other reasons for being in Thunder Canyon than his brother's wedding and more reasons for staying than a pretty blue-eyed bridesmaid.

Pushing all thoughts of Erin Castro from his mind, at least for the time being, he pulled out his laptop and got to work reviewing the reports he needed for his meetings on Wednesday. The information he'd seen so far had been incomplete and often contradictory, warning him that the evaluation he'd expected to finish within a couple of weeks might take a lot longer than that.

At first, he'd been frustrated by this realization, but now—thinking of Erin—the idea of extending his stay in Thunder Canyon didn't bother him at all.

Erin called home on Sunday and spoke to both of her parents. Betty and Jack still didn't know her real reasons for going to Thunder Canyon, but they tried to be supportive of her decision. They asked about her new job and her friends and, as usual, when she would be coming home for a visit.

She had originally planned to go back to San Diego for Thanksgiving, certain she would have all of the answers she sought by then, but she warned her parents now that a trip at that time might not be possible. The holiday was the start of one of the busiest seasons at the resort and she wasn't sure that she would be able to get any time off. But she had another reason for changing her plans—she didn't want to leave Thunder Canyon just when Grant Clifton's sister would be arriving.

She continued to battle against the guilt she felt for not sharing her suspicions with them. She'd never really kept secrets from them before, and certainly never anything of this magnitude—if there could be anything else of such magnitude. Although she'd always felt a little disconnected from her parents and her brothers—as if they shared a deeper bond that somehow eluded her—she'd never been deceitful or dishonest, and the lie that she'd been living for the past several months was weighing heavily on her conscience.

When her mother said, "I love you, Erin," as she always

did at the end of a conversation, Erin's eyes filled with tears.

They *had* always loved her. She didn't doubt that. And she wondered now if the feeling that there was something missing in their relationship was actually indicative of something missing within herself. Maybe she was chasing after something that didn't exist except inside her own imagination.

The original seed had been planted by Erma, but her aunt was gone now and Erin was starting to wonder what purpose could possibly be served by continuing to nurture the old woman's suspicions. And if there was no purpose, then maybe it was time for her to forget everything Erma had said and just go home.

As she readied herself for bed, Erin realized the doubting and confusion had become as much a part of her Sunday night ritual as her call to her parents. Because talking to them inevitably made her realize how much she missed them, and missing them made her question why she was willing to upset the status quo.

Her family wasn't perfect, but they were hers.

Weren't they?

With a sigh, she pulled back the covers and crawled into bed.

As she settled back against her pillows, she acknowledged that it was entirely possible that her birthday being on the same day as Elise Clifton's was nothing more than a coincidence. And both of them being born in the same hospital was probably just another coincidence. But the physical resemblance she'd noticed in Elise's photo and her own brothers was a little harder to ignore.

Or maybe she'd just been looking for answers for so long that she was grasping at straws.

Determined to push these thoughts out of her mind, she

picked up the Stephanie Plum novel she'd just started reading. But she was too distracted to focus on the story and she set the book down again after reading only a few pages.

It took her a long time after that to fall asleep, and when she finally did, she had the strangest dream.

She was in the hospital, and the cry of a baby slowly penetrated the thick fog of pain that surrounded her.

No, not a baby. *Her* baby.

She struggled to sit up but felt as if she was strapped to the bed, unable to move.

"My baby." She tried to shout, but the words were barely a whisper.

"Your baby is fine. We're going to take her to the nursery so that you can rest."

She couldn't see the speaker, but the gentle tone both soothed and reassured her.

A short while later, after she'd rested, she wanted to see her baby. But the hall that led to the nursery seemed to stretch ahead of her forever. She walked faster but made no progress. So she started to run. She ran until her legs were weak and her lungs ached, and still she hadn't reached the end of the long, narrow corridor.

Then suddenly she was there, standing in the middle of the nursery, and her baby was crying again. But there were dozens of bassinets, dozens of crying babies, and she didn't know which one was hers. She ran from one to the next, desperately hoping for some sense of recognition, but they were all the same, all strangers to her.

But then another woman came into the room, and she went directly to one of the bassinets and picked up the crying baby and carried it away. Then another, and another, and another. Until it seemed as if a whole parade of women had come into the room and, one by one, taken away the crying babies until there was only one left.

She tried to rationalize that the one remaining had to be her own, but she wasn't certain. She didn't know how each of the other new mothers had been sure that the baby she was taking belonged to her. What if someone had taken her baby?

She lifted the last infant from its bed, yearning for some sense of connection. But there was nothing. Her eyes scanned the room frantically, searching for someone, anyone, to help her. But she was alone. And when she looked at the baby again, it was gone, too.

Erin awoke with a start. She struggled to sit up and pushed her hair away from her face. Her hands were shaking, her heart was pounding. It was easy to tell herself that it was only a dream. It wasn't so easy to shake the feelings of helplessness and fear that lingered.

There was no reason to believe that the scenario played out by her imagination had any foundation in reality, but she knew that the questions would continue to haunt her until she'd figured out the truth.

Maybe she should go home. Not forever, just for a while. If nothing else, the disturbing dream had proved that she definitely needed a distraction, something to stop her from thinking about hospitals and babies and questions that might never be answered. As if anything could distract her from these thoughts.

Unbidden, an image of Corey Traub came to mind.

Okay, there was a man who could make a woman forget her own name. Just one kiss had proved that. But she wouldn't—couldn't—let him get that close again. She snuggled under the covers, reminding herself that he would probably be heading back to Texas soon anyway, disappearing from her life as abruptly as he'd appeared.

She drifted back to sleep. But this time when she dreamed, she dreamed of Corey.

* * *

Corey wasn't used to chasing women. If anything, he'd become accustomed to being chased by them. Prior to his fifteenth birthday, he'd been short and scrawny and mostly overlooked by everyone. But in that magical year, things had started to change. He'd shot up in height, put on some muscle, started to shave. And when he'd gone out for football the next fall, he'd made the team.

By the time he'd started college, he was a first-string receiver and his family was known across the great state of Texas for the fortune they'd made in oil. Corey had been so caught up in the thrill of being popular that he hadn't questioned what he'd done to earn the attention. Truthfully, the reasons hadn't mattered. All that mattered was that the skinny kid who had been mostly ignored by the girls and laughed at by the older boys was no more.

Corey Traub was now in the spotlight. Guys wanted to hang with him, girls wanted to be seen with him, and he'd reveled in the attention. And then he'd met Heather, and everything had changed. He hadn't needed the adulation of fans so long as he had her attention; he hadn't wanted to be with anyone else so long as he was with her.

They'd dated for a year and a half. She was the first girl he ever loved, and she claimed to love him, too. And then he discovered that, during the entire time they'd been dating, she'd been lying to him, deliberately keeping certain parts of her life a secret from him. When he finally found out and confronted her, she cried and apologized, but learning the extent of her deception had destroyed his trust, and her tears didn't sway him.

It didn't take long for news of their split to make its way around campus, and the girls started coming around again. In the decade that had passed since his college graduation, little had changed. He was as successful in the business world as he'd been on the football field. And although there weren't any shy giggling girls hanging around outside of his locker room, there were plenty of bold, sexy women sneaking into his office after hours or slipping hotel room keys into his pocket.

He couldn't remember the last time he'd had to take the first step with a woman. And it had been a heck of a lot longer than that since any female had told him "no." But somewhere along the line, sometime within the last few years, he'd started to grow weary of empty relationships and meaningless hookups. He wanted what Dillon had found with Erika.

His brothers liked to tease that he fell in love too easily, but the truth was, Heather's deception had taught him to be careful with his heart. Not that he'd given up on falling in love. He was still hopeful that would happen, but the next time he opened up his heart completely, it would be to a woman who he could trust was capable of loving him the same way. Openly and honestly, without any secrets or lies between them.

There was something about Erin Castro that made him think she might be that woman.

Maybe he was putting the cart before the horse, considering that she hadn't even agreed to have lunch with him. But he refused to be dissuaded. If he'd believed that she was honestly not interested, he would have backed off. But he couldn't forget the way she'd looked at him when they danced, the way she'd trembled in his arms, the way she'd responded to his kiss. No way was the attraction one-sided.

When Monday morning came around and he still hadn't managed to put her out of his mind, he decided to track her down. Because he was staying in one of the resort's condo units, it would be easy enough to stop by the front desk of the main building and invite her to lunch and see where things went from there. Except that when he went down to the desk, he didn't see her anywhere.

"Erin isn't in today," Trina told him.

"Will she be in later?" he asked, wondering if she'd switched her shift for some reason.

"I doubt it. She called in sick."

Sick?

He knew she hadn't been feeling well Saturday night, but she'd sounded okay when he'd spoken with her Sunday morning. Did she have a touch of the flu or some other kind of bug and had suffered a relapse?

"Is there something I can help you with?" Trina's long lashes fluttered, the invitation in those green eyes obvious.

"No, thanks," he told her. "I'll catch up with Erin later."

"If you change your mind, you can catch up with me around four." Her glossy pink lips curved. "That's when I finish my shift."

"I'll remember that," he told her, determined to ensure that he was nowhere around when Trina got off work.

With any luck, he would be with Erin.

Erin prided herself on being a reliable employee, someone who could be depended on to get things done, whatever those things might be. But when she woke up Monday morning and still hadn't figured out what—if anything—to say to her boss about her suspicion that he might be her brother, she called in sick.

When her bell rang shortly after 10:00 a.m., she didn't think twice before responding to the summons. It wasn't until she'd peeked through the sidelight and saw Corey on her step, making her heart do a little hop and skip, that she hesitated. Unfortunately, he was looking through the same window from the other side, which meant there was no way she could now pretend she wasn't home.

Forcing a smile, she pulled open the door.

"Corey, hi."

He smiled back, and she felt that funny little quiver in her belly again.

"I stopped by the resort to see you, and Trina said you were home sick," he explained. His gaze skimmed over her, leisurely, appraisingly. "But you look pretty good to me."

"I wasn't feeling well when I got up this morning," she fibbed, conscious that her cheeks were burning. "I thought I should stay home…in case I was contagious."

"Well, I brought you some homemade chicken soup—my mother's favorite cure for whatever ails you."

"*You* made chicken soup?"

He chuckled at the obvious skepticism in her tone. "No, I bought chicken soup that was homemade by the wonderful chefs at the Gallatin Room."

She lifted a brow at his mention of the resort's fine dining restaurant and figured the little plastic bowl in his hand probably cost more than a whole meal at any other restaurant in town.

"Thank you," she said. "That was a really sweet gesture."

"But you've already had lunch," he guessed.

She nodded.

"So put it in the fridge for tomorrow."

It would be rude to refuse his offer, so she did as he suggested, though she wondered what kind of strings might be attached to the bowl in her hand.

"Thank you," she said again. "I'm sure I'll enjoy it."

"What are your plans for the afternoon? Because I know you're not working."

"I have no plans. I'm home sick," she reminded him.

His smile widened. "Don't worry. I won't turn you in for playing hooky…so long as you let me play hooky with you."

"You're blackmailing me?"

He shrugged. "Whatever works."

"What did you have in mind?" she asked warily.

"Just grab a jacket and put on a pair of boots."

Which, of course, told her absolutely nothing about what he had planned. "Look, Corey, I'm flattered that you'd go to such lengths to spend time with me, but I really don't understand why."

"There's nothing to understand. I just think some time outside in the crisp, fresh air will help you feel better," he assured her.

"I don't know," she hedged.

"Trust me."

It wasn't that she didn't trust Corey so much as she didn't trust herself to be alone with him. The attraction she felt whenever she was near him was both awesome and over-whelming.

As she went to get her jacket and boots, she couldn't help but think he looked as relaxed and unself-conscious in the jeans and flannel he was wearing today as he had in the designer tux he'd worn for his brother's wedding, making her curious to know which was the *real* Corey Traub. Not that it mattered. Her instinctive response to him was the same regardless of what he was wearing.

She didn't understand the attraction. She'd always dated guys who were…more subtle, she decided. There was noth-ing subtle about Corey. He was blatantly and undeniably male.

And the way he filled out a pair of jeans made her want to sigh. The cowboy boots didn't surprise her. He'd even worn a pair at the wedding, with his tux. But those boots had been polished, and these were battered and worn, like the hat on his head.

She'd never known a cowboy before she came to Montana. And even in the past few months, she'd never met anyone like Corey.

He wasn't just sexy. He was knock-the-breath-out-of-your-lungs sexy. And the way he smiled at her, he knew it.

She'd never liked arrogant men. Or maybe it was just that she'd always wondered why the men she'd known felt entitled to their arrogance. With Corey, there was no question of his entitlement. And it made her wonder, not for the first time, why he was interested in her.

She wasn't oblivious to her own appeal. Over the years, she'd received a fair share of compliments on her appearance, and she knew how to play up her attributes—how to apply makeup so her blue eyes looked bluer, how to dress so that her curves seemed curvier, how to walk into a room so that heads turned in her direction.

Since coming to Thunder Canyon, however, she'd deliberately downplayed her appearance. She'd toned down her makeup and dressed to blend in rather than stand out. No one looked at her twice, and no one asked any questions. At least, not until Erika's wedding.

When Erin agreed to be a bridesmaid, she'd been thinking that she could somehow hide beneath layers of pink organza ruffles. She should have remembered that her friend had exquisite taste and an eye for fashion. There had been no way to hide in the strapless satin gown that hugged her curves. And she could hardly refuse when the bride suggested that her maid of honor should have her hair and makeup professionally done.

The result was that, as she'd made her way up the aisle,

she'd been aware of the attention focused on her—and the speculation. She recognized some of her regular customers from the Hitching Post who had never looked twice when she'd waited on their tables and others who she'd met through her duties at the resort. None of them seemed to realize who she was. And although she'd been all too aware that the groom's brother wasn't the only man who had been watching her, he was the only one she'd watched back.

Corey snapped his phone shut when Erin came back with her jacket and boots.

"Everything's arranged," he told her.

"What is *everything?*"

"You'll find out soon enough."

"I don't like surprises," she warned, following him out the door.

"Everyone likes surprises," he insisted.

She shook her head as she turned her key in the lock, engaging the deadbolt.

He slid an arm across her shoulders and steered her toward his truck. "What happened, darlin'? Were you traumatized by a clown jumping out of your cake on your fifth birthday?"

"Nothing so dramatic. I just like to have a plan, and I don't like when things interfere with my plans."

He opened the passenger-side door for her. "Didn't John Lennon say something about life being what happens while you're making other plans?"

"Maybe that worked for him," she acknowledged, "but it's a strange philosophy for a management consultant."

"It's not my business philosophy," he told her. "But when I'm out of the office, I don't like being shackled by rules and schedules."

She stepped up into the truck, obviously thinking about

his response. He closed her door, then went around to the driver's side.

"My aunt died," she finally said.

He paused in the act of inserting the key into the ignition. "Today? Is that why you called into work?"

She shook her head. "No. A few months ago." She folded her hands, staring down at the fingers linked together in her lap. "You asked why I don't like surprises. Her death was a surprise. And she gave me some information just before she passed that was...unexpected. I had so many questions that I never got to ask her."

"I'm sorry," he said. "I know how hard it is to lose someone out of the blue, feeling as if you'd left something unresolved."

She looked at him, as if surprised by his response. "Who did you lose?"

"My father."

"I didn't realize—" She frowned. "I should have. When you introduced your mother and her husband, I just assumed your parents were divorced."

He shook his head. "My dad died in an explosion on an oil rig when I was eight. The last time I saw him, before he went to work that day, he swatted my butt for talking back to my mother. When he walked out the door, I was happy to see him go."

She touched a hand to his arm, and when she spoke, her voice was gentle. "You were eight," she reminded him.

"I know. I got over the guilt a long time ago but only after I'd carried it around for a lot of years first." He frowned.

Her hand dropped away. "What's wrong?"

"I was just thinking that it's mighty easy to talk to you."

"It is?"

"I haven't ever told anyone that story. Not anyone outside of the family, anyway."

"Sometimes it's easier to talk to someone who isn't close to a situation."

He turned into the long, winding drive that led to the Hopping H Ranch. "And sometimes a man just doesn't have the sense to hold his tongue around a beautiful woman."

Her cheeks flushed. "I might be a California girl, but I've heard plenty of stories about you smooth-talking cowboys to know that I'd be a fool to trust even half of the words that slide off of that glib tongue."

He pressed a hand to his heart as he pulled into a vacant parking spot. "Now you've wounded me."

The look of patent disbelief that she aimed in his direction changed to something more akin to wariness when she realized where he'd brought her.

Chapter Four

"This is Melanie and Russ's ranch."

Though it wasn't a question, Corey nodded anyway.

"What are we doing here?"

"I would have thought that was obvious." He got out of the truck and came around to her side.

This time Erin hadn't jumped out ahead of him. In fact, she didn't look like she had any intention of getting out at all. She hadn't even unfastened her seatbelt, so he reached across to release the clasp for her.

"This isn't a good idea," she said.

"Why not?"

"Because I already missed work today. I don't want to miss tomorrow, too, because I'm in a body cast in the hospital."

"You can't ride?" He deliberately infused his tone with both surprise and disbelief and a hint of challenge.

"Of course, I can ride," she said, then added, "waves."

"Waves?"

"I grew up on the coast, not in cowboy country," she reminded him.

The mention of surfing had distracted him with thoughts of Erin clad in a skimpy little bikini, her hair slicked back, her skin wet and glistening as she balanced on a longboard. He knew it was more likely that she wore a wetsuit and figured she'd probably look just as enticing in a full bodysuit of neoprene that hugged her feminine curves, but a man was entitled to his fantasies and Erin in a bikini was definitely one of his. Peeling the little scraps of fabric from her damp skin was another.

"Well, you're in cowboy country now," he said, forcing the all-too tempting images from his mind.

"I'm aware of that," she said, just as Russ came out of the barn.

The rancher came over to shake hands with Corey and Erin.

"Thanks for accommodating us," Corey said.

"Always a pleasure," Russ assured him.

Erin remained silent, wary.

"I've got Lucifer and Jax all saddled up and ready to go, but you just let me know if you need anything else."

"Will do," Corey promised.

And Russ disappeared into the barn again.

"Lucifer?"

Corey pointed out the spirited black stallion in a nearby enclosure. "And here—" he guided her to a closer paddock "—is Jax."

She hesitated a few feet from the fence.

"You've never ridden before?" He couldn't imagine going through life without experiencing the exhilarating freedom of racing over the open fields on the back of a horse.

"No, I have." Her gaze flickered cautiously toward the horse again. "Twice."

"When you were a kid?"

She shook her head. "A few weeks ago."

His lips twitched as he fought a smile. "What happened?"

"Haley convinced me that I couldn't live in Montana if I didn't know how to ride, so I decided to take some private lessons."

"And you had two?"

"I *suffered* through each one and decided the bruises on my butt were never going to go away if I kept them up."

Corey shook his head. "You don't strike me as the type of woman to give up so easily."

"You don't know me," she reminded him.

"I'm working on it."

"And accepting that something isn't working doesn't equal giving up."

"It sure sounds like giving up to me."

"If you came here to ride, go ahead," she said. "Don't worry about me."

"And what will you do?"

"I can watch."

He curved an arm around her shoulders and guided her closer to the docile bay gelding. He whistled softly, and the horse ambled over to the fence.

Erin looked at Jax.

It was an innocuous-sounding name, and the animal seemed well behaved, but he was just so big. Okay, not quite as big as Lucifer, and certainly not anywhere near as menacing as the powerful stallion that was pawing impatiently at the ground and tossing his head from side to side, but still pretty intimidating. But there was something about those big dark eyes that encouraged her to trust that, though he was big and strong enough to toss her around like a rag doll, he wouldn't.

She started to reach toward the horse, testing herself as much as the animal, then hesitated.

Corey caught her wrist before she could withdraw and guided her hand the rest of the way, until her palm was flat against the horse's neck. She felt the muscles quiver beneath her touch, and the gelding blew out a quiet breath that sounded distinctly like a sigh of pleasure.

Corey's hand dropped away, but he remained close while she continued to stroke the animal.

"I think he likes me," Erin told him.

He smiled. "Of course he likes you. He'd like you even more if you took him out for the run he's saddled up for."

Still, she hesitated.

"It's okay if you're afraid."

Her shoulders stiffened. "I'm not afraid."

His lips curved, just a little, and she knew that she'd fallen straight into his trap. He vaulted easily over the fence, then put one foot in the stirrup and swung himself into the saddle, then he held out his hand to her. "Come on."

Erin remained rooted where she was. "I thought you were going to ride Lucifer."

"I am," he said. "We're just going to take a walk around the paddock together, until you're comfortable with Jax."

Still she hesitated. "You expect me to get up on that horse with you?"

"You won't fall off," he promised.

"Won't we be too heavy for the horse?"

"We're just going to take a few turns around the paddock. He can handle it."

Erin remained skeptical.

"Trust me, darlin', I know what these animals are worth and I wouldn't do anything to risk harming any of them."

"Maybe I'm more worried about harm to me," she told him, but climbed up onto the fence—keeping a wary eye on the horse—and over.

"I won't let anything happen to you." He smiled. "Not anything that you don't want to happen, that is."

It was as much an enticement as a warning. She felt her cheeks flush but chose to ignore the innuendo.

She thought she was going to fall off before she ever managed to get on, but eventually she managed to climb up, straddling the horse's back behind the saddle.

"Put your arms around me and hold on," he told her.

She did so, all too aware of his solid warmth and masculine strength. His jacket was unzipped and she could feel the ripple of his muscles beneath the soft fabric of his shirt. Her mouth went dry—although whether it was from fear of the horse or awareness of Corey, she wasn't certain.

He nudged Jax into motion, and as Erin felt herself starting to slide, she fisted her hands in Corey's shirt and held on for dear life. He only chuckled. As the horse made its way around the paddock and she realized how easily he was controlling the powerful animal with the hard muscles of his thighs, her grip on the flannel gradually loosened.

Her own muscles felt watery; her limbs were weak. And her heart was pounding so hard inside her chest she was surprised he couldn't hear it. The rocking motion was somewhat familiar, and the familiarity made her tense. Her butt was definitely going to be sore tomorrow, and the knowledge made her wish that she'd never responded to Corey's knock on her door. She really did want to learn to ride, but maybe she just wasn't cut out to be a horsewoman.

"Relax."

She did and realized that when she stopped trying to anticipate the horse's movements, she didn't jolt up and down so much. In fact, she could almost enjoy the steady, easy rhythm. Lulled by this discovery, she closed her eyes and pressed her cheek against Corey's back, breathing in the heady scent of leather and horse and man.

She felt the familiar stir of desire low in her belly, and a tingling warmth between her thighs. Obviously as her worry lessened, her awareness heightened. With every step the horse took, her breasts brushed against Corey's back, and she was suddenly aware that her nipples had tightened into hard points that were straining against her bra, aching for much more intimate contact.

She wanted his hands on her, stroking over her bare skin, touching her everywhere.

He glanced over his shoulder. "Ready for more?"

She wondered, for a moment, if she'd said something out loud, but then she realized that he was referring to the horse's pace, and she nodded.

A nudge of his knees against the horse's flank and the animal moved from a jog to a canter—if she was remembering the terms correctly—and suddenly every nerve ending in her body was on high alert. She'd never found the experience of being on horseback anything but scary and awkward and painful, but with Corey it was exhilarating and incredible and sensuous.

It had been obvious to Corey that Erin had some apprehension about getting up on a horse again, so riding with her seemed like the perfect way to ease her worries. It had worked with his sister, Rose. When she was little, she'd fallen off the back of her pony and had been terrified to climb back up again. But she'd trusted her big brother, and riding with Corey had given her the courage to overcome her fears.

It didn't take a minute for Corey to realize that sharing a horse with a grown woman was a very different experience than doing so with his six-year-old sister. And when that woman was soft and sexy and snuggled up behind him, it was sheer torture.

Only for a few trips around the paddock, he promised himself, then she would be ready to handle Jax on her own—or Jax would be ready to handle her. The horse had a gentle nature and was well-trained, both essential qualities for the mount of a novice rider. He didn't know where Erin had gone for her lessons, but for her to have thrown in the towel after only two sessions, she'd either been given a difficult horse or had a horrible instructor. He was determined not to let that memory prevent her from enjoying the day.

He wanted to share this experience with her, to introduce her to pleasures that no one else ever had. And he wasn't just thinking about what they could do on horseback.

And while he tried to keep a tight rein on his thoughts, it was next to impossible. He was all too aware of her arms around him, of her soft breasts pressed to his back, rubbing against him. Though he was sure he couldn't actually feel the hard nubs of her nipples through the layers that separated them, he imagined that he could. He wanted to touch her, all of her. He wanted to strip away her clothes and—

He managed to lasso the runaway fantasy before it took him to the point of no return and, after another torturously slow turn around the paddock, he said, "Let's see what you can do on your own."

They headed out at a leisurely gait. Surprisingly, after half an hour in the paddock with Corey and Jax, Erin felt a lot more comfortable on the back of the horse than she had at any time during her two lessons. She had a moment of panic when they headed away from the barn, but Jax was so strong and steady beneath her that it was gone as quickly as it had come.

Lucifer wasn't nearly as complacent, and though Corey didn't have any trouble controlling the spirited stallion, it was obvious that the animal was eager to run. His feet danced impatiently and he tossed his head excitedly, but Corey held him in check and continued to keep pace with Erin and Jax.

When they broke through a stand of trees to yet another open field, Erin said, "Why don't you let him run?"

Corey looked over his shoulder. "I don't want to leave you."

"Well, I would appreciate it if you came back."

He grinned at her dry tone. "Are you sure you don't mind?"

"I'm sure," she said. "And I'm guessing that you crave the speed as much as he does."

He didn't deny it. "We'll be back."

She knew they would. And truthfully, she didn't mind letting them go. In fact, it was a pleasure to watch them streak across the fields. Horse and rider—two beautiful beings—so closely attuned to one another they moved as if they were one entity. As they raced off into the distance, Erin sighed.

What was she doing? She had no business being here with this man, no reason to think that getting involved with him could end up in anything but heartache. He was from Texas, she was from California, and it was only a coincidence that their paths happened to cross in Montana. She didn't even know how long he planned to stay in Thunder Canyon—or even how long she did.

But why couldn't she enjoy his company so long as he was here? For once in her life, why couldn't she be impulsive and irresponsible and just let things happen?

She heard them returning before she saw them. The thunderous pounding of the stallion's hooves in the distance made her turn just as they plunged through a copse of towering pines. The horse raced ahead, wild and reckless, and the man on its back looked every bit as dangerous. But it wasn't fear that made Erin's heart pound in her chest—it was excitement. Anticipation. Lust.

She wanted him. It was ridiculous to continue to deny it. It was also ridiculous to imagine that she could ever have him for anything more than a very hot, very short-term fling.

And what would be so wrong about that? her clamoring hormones demanded to know.

As he drew nearer, her heart pounded even harder.

What would be wrong, she reminded herself sternly, *was that she didn't even know the man.* Aside from the fact that he was Dillon's brother, she knew almost nothing about him. And she wasn't in the habit of falling into bed with men she didn't know.

Corey reined in the horse, reducing his pace to a canter, then a trot and finally slowing him to a walk as they approached Erin and Jax. She turned her mount around and began to head back, but she was less successful in redirecting her thoughts.

"You both look as if you enjoyed that," Erin said.

"I don't think there's anything I love more than exploring the great outdoors on horseback."

"This is beautiful country," she agreed.

"The prettiest in the whole world, apart from Texas, of course."

"Of course," she agreed drily.

He grinned. "Although I hear the West Coast has some good stuff, too. Like California girls."

"Are you going to break into song now?"

"I only ever sing in the shower," he told her, "so if you want to be serenaded—"

"Not necessary," she assured him.

Corey chuckled.

"So what did you think?" he asked a few minutes later. "Not just of the ranch, but the ride."

"I think I could learn to like this," she admitted.

"I knew you would," he said confidently.

There was that arrogance again—but it definitely suited him.

"You've probably been riding since you were little," she guessed.

"Since I was knee high to a grasshopper, to hear my mama tell the story."

She made a point of tilting her head way back to look up at him. "I can't imagine you were ever knee high to a grasshopper."

"I was," he surprised her by admitting. "In fact, I was short and scrawny almost all the way through high school. I couldn't even get a date to my junior prom."

"And your senior prom?"

He grinned. "Well, that was a different story."

"I'll bet."

"How about you? Did you go to your senior prom?"

She thought back, smiled. "Yes, I did. I went with Thomas Anderson. He was president of the chess club, editor of the yearbook, valedictorian of our graduating class."

"The first boy you ever slept with?" he prompted.

She shook her head. "No. But he was the first boy to break my heart."

"Where is he now? Want me to go beat him up?"

She laughed. "That's not necessary. I got over him a long time ago."

"Glad to hear that," he said. "How about more recently?"

"More recently what?"

"Have you been dating anyone in Thunder Canyon?"

"No. And I'm not looking to start, either."

"Why not?"

She shrugged. "I've been working a lot."

"You know what they say about all work and no play," he warned her.

"I don't play games."

"Some games are fun, darlin'."

She smiled at that, but her smile quickly faded. "I was dating someone in San Diego for a while."

"Did he break your heart, too?"

She shook her head. "But I think I might have bruised his."

"And you're still feeling guilty about it," he guessed.

"Maybe. I don't know. I didn't think our relationship was that serious. We hadn't been dating very long, but he was looking to make a commitment and I wasn't."

"Because you're not ready to settle down? Or because you didn't want to settle down with him?"

"I just didn't want to settle," she said and winced when she realized how the words sounded.

But Corey nodded, understanding. "There was something missing."

"A lot of somethings, actually," she admitted.

"How is that your fault?"

"Well, according to my mother, I didn't give him a chance, my expectations are too high, I need to understand that chemistry takes time—" she broke off, her cheeks burning. "Well, that's getting a lot more personal than I meant to."

"So, there was no chemistry with this guy, huh?"

She ignored his question because she knew the answer would lead her down a treacherous path.

They were at the barn now, and Corey dismounted before turning to help Erin down. She was grateful for his assistance, because as relaxed as she'd begun to feel in the saddle she wasn't at all confident in her ability to get out of it. She put her hands on his shoulders and slid down, the front of her body brushing against the front of his.

Like flint rubbing against rock, sparks flashed, heat flared. Her breath caught, her pulse pounded. His hands stayed on her hips, holding her close.

And suddenly she was smack in the middle of that treacherous path she'd been so determined to avoid.

"Did you guys have a good time?" Russ asked.

Erin jumped back, her cheeks burning.

"Oh, yes," she said. "It was wonderful. Thank you."

"Not a problem," Russ said. "Melanie's just about to put dinner on the table. There's plenty of food, if you wanted to join us."

"Oh." She wasn't sure how to respond to the invitation. She'd met Russ and Melanie a few times and didn't want to refuse his generous offer, but she wasn't sure she'd feel comfortable sitting down at a table with people she barely knew.

"Thanks for the invite," Corey said, coming to her rescue. "But Erin and I have other plans."

"You're sure?" Russ pressed.

"Positive. But please thank Melanie for us."

His friend nodded. "I will. And I hope you'll find your way out here again before you head back to Texas."

"You can count on it," Corey said, shaking his hand firmly.

The rancher tipped his hat to Erin, then led the horses into the barn.

* * *

"How are you holding up?" Corey asked when they were back in his truck and heading away from the ranch.

"Not too badly," she said.

"You should take a hot bath before you go to bed tonight," he suggested. "It will help ease any soreness in your muscles."

"That sounds like a wonderful idea." She tipped her head back and closed her eyes as if she was imagining herself sinking into a tub filled with bubbles.

Or maybe he just assumed that was what was on her mind because it was on his.

"And if it doesn't work, I'll call Stefan in the morning and see if he can squeeze me in for a quickie during my lunch."

"Stefan? A quickie?"

She laughed. "A quick massage," she clarified.

"Oh." But his frown deepened. "Don't they have women who give massages?"

"Of course. But Stefan has the most amazing hands."

"And you let him put them all over your body?"

"I pay him to put them all over my body." She didn't usually engage in this kind of flirtatious banter, but Corey's reaction to her statement was so typically and possessively male, she couldn't resist teasing him a little. "And he's worth every penny."

"I could do the same thing—for free."

She lifted a brow. "Show me your diploma, cowboy."

"Well, no one's ever called it a diploma, but—"

She laughed. "I was referring to a professional accreditation. Stefan trained in Sweden."

"I graduated from Texas A&M," he said, flicking on his indicator.

Instead of heading in the direction Erin lived, he turned the opposite way.

"Where are we going?" she asked, more curious than concerned.

"I told Russ we had plans for dinner," he reminded her. "You don't want to make a liar out of me, do you?"

"I just don't want you to feel obligated—"

"Erin."

She frowned at the interruption.

"You seem to be forgetting that I'm the one who tracked you down this morning and pretty much blackmailed you into spending the day with me."

"You did, didn't you?"

"Which should prove that if I didn't want to be with you, I wouldn't be."

"Okay," she finally said, but the furrow in her brow deepened when he pulled into the parking lot of the Super Saver Mart, still referred to by a lot of the locals as the Thunder Canyon Mercantile. "This is where we're going for dinner?"

He chuckled. "This is where we're going to get the ingredients for dinner."

She looked at him suspiciously.

"No, I don't expect you to cook dinner for me," he said before she could ask. "I'm going to cook for you."

"You are?"

"Why do you sound so surprised?"

"I guess because I am," she admitted, as they made their way toward the entrance. "No man has ever cooked me dinner before."

He eyed her warily. "Are you one of those—what do they call them—vegetarians or vegans or whatever?"

The tone of his voice left her in no doubt what this man

from cattle country thought of that possibility and made her lips curve. "No, I'm not a vegetarian or a vegan."

"Are you a picky eater?"

"There are some things I don't like," she admitted, "but I'm not picky."

"What don't you like?"

"Peas. Pickles. Pineapple."

He lifted his brows. "You have something against the letter 'p'?"

"I don't like squash, either."

"Like...pumpkin?"

She smiled again. "Any kind of squash."

"Well then, I think we're pretty safe," he told her. "Because there are no peas, pickles, pineapple or squash in my red sauce."

"I do like red sauce."

"How do you feel about pasta?"

"I love pasta."

He grinned. "Then let's go shopping."

Chapter Five

If she'd been surprised by his offer to cook for her, she was even more so by the ease with which he pushed the cart around the grocery store. He didn't just toss the vegetables into a bag, he checked the color of the tomatoes, tested the firmness of the garlic, gauged the texture of the peppers.

She made a face when he was sniffing the mushrooms. "Those aren't one of my favorite foods," she admitted to him.

"These are shiitake, not porcini," he teased.

"I'm just not a fan of any kind of fungus," she said.

"You won't even taste them."

She decided to give him the benefit of the doubt. After all, she was going to sit down for a home-cooked meal that she didn't have to prepare, and she was curious about his skill in the kitchen. Okay, she was curious about his skill in other areas, too, but she refused to let her mind go down that path. Again.

He added a head of romaine lettuce, a bag of carrots, a bunch of green onions and a cucumber.

Moving out of the produce department to the bakery, he grabbed a loaf of French bread, then a package of fresh fettucine, extra virgin olive oil, basil, oregano, a hunk of parmesan cheese and a bottle of red wine.

"You've thought of everything, haven't you?"

He took a mental inventory of the ingredients as they moved along the conveyor belt toward the cashier. "I hope so."

"Do you do this often?"

"Shop for groceries?"

"Cook."

"Do you mean cook for a woman or just cook in general?"

"Cook in general," she said, unwilling to admit that she was just as curious to know if he was in the habit of cooking for his female companions.

"I have to eat," he said logically.

"But—" She bit her lip, stifling the reply that had almost spilled out uncensored.

"But," he prompted.

She felt her cheeks burn. "I just thought you'd probably have women lining up to cook for you."

"Well, if you're offering …" He grinned.

"You said you were cooking for me," she reminded him.

"Tonight," he agreed. "But maybe next time you could show off your culinary skills."

"You're assuming there will be a next time."

"Not assuming," he denied. "Just hopeful."

She had enjoyed the time they'd spent together today and, so long as he wasn't looking for anything more than friendship from her—and so long as she remembered that she wasn't in a position to offer anything more—she wouldn't object to spending more time with him.

"I do make a mean enchilada," she told him.

"Spicy?"

"I guess I'll let you be the judge of that."

"I'll look forward to it." He smiled before he turned to the cashier to pay for his groceries.

Corey put Erin to work washing the lettuce and other vegetables while he got busy chopping and dicing. Her kitchen was laid out almost identical to the one in the condo he was renting, so he felt comfortable moving around in it and opening cupboards and drawers to find what he needed. He located a big pot to boil water for the pasta and a wok-style frying pan that he could use to make the sauce. He opened the bottle of wine to let it breathe while he heated a drizzle of olive oil in the pan and tossed in a couple of crushed garlic cloves.

"Where did you learn to cook?" Erin asked him.

He dumped the red and green peppers into the pan, stirred them around with a wooden spoon, then began peeling the tomatoes.

"Here and there," he said.

She lifted her brows at the vagueness of his response, but he didn't elaborate. He didn't think he'd score any points with Erin by admitting it was an ex-girlfriend who'd taught him the basics of the sauce he was currently making for her. Especially not if she knew that he'd appreciated Gina's marinara sauce more than he'd appreciated Gina and, once he'd realized that, he'd decided to learn to make it for himself so that he could enjoy his pasta without the complications of an unhappy relationship.

"Why don't you pour the wine?" he suggested.

She found two glasses in the cupboard and did as he suggested.

He finished dicing the tomatoes he'd peeled and tossed them into the pan, then added some spices and stirred everything around again.

"It smells good already," Erin told him.

He washed his hands and dried them on the towel that was hanging over the handle of the oven door before he turned to take the glass of wine she offered to him. "It will taste even better," he promised.

Her brows rose up again. "Cocky, aren't you?"

"Confident," he corrected.

When he stepped toward her, Erin felt an instinctual urge to retreat. But the counter was at her back, leaving her with nowhere to go.

His lips curved, slowly, seductively. Her heart hammered.

She had no doubt that he had reason to be confident. She knew enough about his background to know that he'd been born into a powerful and influential family, but he'd also achieved his own success. And men like Corey, men who wore success and self-assurance as comfortably as the designer labels on their backs, drew more than their fair share of female attention. Which made her wonder—what was he doing with her?

She wasn't oblivious to her own appeal, but she wasn't an heiress or a supermodel, and she didn't doubt that Corey had dated women from each of those categories—and a few more. She also guessed that he was a man accustomed to getting what he wanted, and the look in his eyes left her in no doubt that what he wanted, at least right now, was her. And though she had no intention of giving in to the desire that surged through her veins, she couldn't deny that she wanted him right back.

His gaze dropped to her mouth, and she knew that if he kissed her again, right here and right now, she would be lost. She put a hand out—a desperate, wordless attempt to hold him off, at least long enough for her to gather her wits about her—and realized she was holding her glass of wine in it.

"Well, then," she said, lifting her glass a little higher. "We should toast to dinner."

Amusement crinkled the corners of his eyes as he tapped the rim of his glass against hers.

"To dinner," he agreed, "with new friends."

She sipped her wine without tasting it, all too aware of his closeness and the intensity of his gaze on her.

"I should set the table."

"There's no rush," he assured her. "The sauce needs to simmer for about half an hour."

Half an hour?

It wasn't all that long, really, but somehow, it seemed like an eternity. Because the more time she spent with Corey, the more difficult it was to ignore the attraction she felt.

Her immediate response to him had been purely physical—the first time they met, she hadn't known him well enough for it to be anything more than a hormonal response to a good-looking man who practically oozed charm and sex appeal. But the more she got to know Corey, the more she found herself actually liking him.

Despite the attraction that zinged between them, she felt comfortable with him. Comfortable enough to laugh when he teased her, to respond in kind when he flirted with her and to enjoy the conversations they shared as much as the silences that sometimes fell in-between. Yeah, she was definitely starting to like him, and the combination of lust and like was a lot more difficult to ignore than a purely hormonal reaction.

But when they were alone together, as they were now, the pleasure she felt in his company grew into more, and she wasn't completely comfortable with that.

"Speaking of the sauce," she said, needing to break the spell that had woven around her like a spider's web, invisibly drawing her closer to him. And just like a fly caught in a web, she knew that it would be dangerous to let him get any closer.

"What about the sauce?" There was a hint of laughter in his voice, amusement sparkling in his eyes.

"Don't you need to stir it…or something?"

"Or something," he agreed and lifted a hand to trail a finger down her cheek.

Her pulse pounded, her breath caught.

Corey's eyes stayed locked with hers.

"You're a bundle of contradictions, Erin Castro."

She didn't dare ask what he meant, or maybe she was afraid that she knew. As clearly as she could read the desire in his eyes, she was sure he could see the same want echoed in hers. But she'd told him that she didn't want to get involved, and she'd meant it.

"I'm not trying to be," she told him.

He held her gaze for another minute before he stepped back. "I know. And that's why I'm going to focus on my sauce and let you set the table."

She exhaled slowly and turned to set her wineglass on the counter. As she reached into the cupboard for the plates, she assured herself that she was grateful he'd backed away.

Grateful and relieved.

And more than a little disappointed.

Half an hour later, they were seated at the table enjoying hot pasta, warm bread and crisp salad.

"You were right," she admitted. "It tastes even better than it smells—and it smells fabulous."

He twirled his fork in his own pasta. "I'm glad you're enjoying it."

"Are you kidding? This is one of the best meals I've had since…" Her words trailed off.

Since she'd come to Thunder Canyon, she suddenly realized and felt a pang of sadness thinking of the family she'd left in San Diego. But she'd had no choice. Not if she wanted to find the answers to the questions that Erma had planted in her mind. And she did want those answers. She *needed* the answers in order to understand who she really was.

"Since?" Corey prompted.

She forced a smile. "Since I can't remember when," she told him, keeping her voice deliberately light. "Really, this is amazing."

He took a slice of warm bread from the basket, tore it in half. "Do you want to talk about it?"

She swallowed another mouthful of pasta, then wiped her mouth with her napkin. "Talk about what?"

"Whatever's on your mind."

She reached for her wineglass. "There's nothing—"

He touched a finger to her lips, halting the automatic denial. She set her glass back down, nearly sloshing wine over the rim.

"If you don't want to talk about it, say so, darlin'," he told her. "But don't tell me there's nothing because it was obvious when I got here this morning that there was something bothering you and I can tell that your thoughts are wandering again."

She wondered if she'd been so obviously preoccupied or if he was more intuitive than she would have guessed. Either way, she couldn't imagine telling him what she'd been thinking. She couldn't imagine telling *anyone* about her suspicions, though she knew she should probably talk to someone before she took the next step.

Right now she had no idea what her next step was going to be, how to follow-up and find proof of her theory. Sure, she'd considered approaching Grant and saying, "I think I might be your sister." But as hard as she tried, she couldn't imagine how he might respond to such an announcement, except that she was confident he would *not* throw his arms around her and say, "Welcome to the family."

At the very least, he would be cautious; more likely, suspicious; possibly he would even question her sanity. All of which would be understandable reactions to such an unexpected claim, and all of which reaffirmed for Erin her decision to stay away from the resort today and avoid any chance of crossing paths with her boss.

But as much as her actions had been motivated by self-preservation, she couldn't deny that she was glad Corey had shown up and taken her mind off of the situation—at least for a while.

"I was just thinking that I was glad I played hooky today," she told him, because that was true.

His eyes narrowed, as if he knew she wasn't being completely truthful with him, but then he smiled. "I'm glad you played hooky today, too."

"Unfortunately, I can't keep playing hooky, which means that I have an early morning." She pushed her chair away from the table and stood up, taking her plate and cutlery to the dishwasher.

"Is that supposed to be my cue to take off?"

"Yes, it is," she said, but with more than a hint of reluctance.

She really had enjoyed her day with Corey—and she'd appreciated that he'd been able to take her mind off of her worries when nothing and no one else had done so.

"I'll head out as soon as the kitchen is cleared up," he told her.

"You cooked dinner, so I'll take care of the cleanup."

"That doesn't seem fair when I made the mess."

"It's more than fair, considering the delicious meal I just ate."

"Are you sure?"

"I'm sure." More importantly, she was worried that if she didn't get him out of her apartment as soon as possible, she might change her mind about wanting him to go.

"All right then," he relented. "But only because I have some early morning meetings myself that I need to prepare for."

"Meetings? I didn't realize…I thought you were just in town for your brother's wedding."

"I would have come just for the wedding," he agreed. "But as it turned out, I had a business opportunity come up in the area."

"Then you're going to be staying in Thunder Canyon for a while?"

He leaned closer. "Do you want me to?"

More than she should, and that was *not* an admission she was willing to make to a man who was all too aware of the effect he had on the female species. Instead, she only said, "I'm sure your plans have nothing to do with me."

His smile, slow and sexy, made her heart bump against her ribs.

"Don't be too sure, darlin'," he said in a tone that was as slow and sexy as his smile and shimmered over her skin like a caress. "While it's true that some new opportunities have come up, I'm not sure I would have been so willing to hang around if I wasn't also tempted by the possibility of spending some more time with you."

"I told you—" she had to look away to break the hypnotic

effect of those espresso-colored eyes "—I'm not looking to get involved with anyone right now."

"Yeah, you told me," he agreed. "But your kisses say somethin' totally different, darlin'."

"It was one kiss—and it never should have happened."

"My mama might have raised me to be a gentleman," he said, "but she also taught me to never back down from a challenge."

"That wasn't a challenge," she said.

"Wasn't it?"

"No," she insisted vehemently, desperately. "It was a statement of fact."

He smiled again. "We'll see about that, darlin'."

"And stop calling me *darlin'*."

"My apologies…Erin."

The way he spoke her name made it sound more intimate than any words of passion that had ever been whispered between lovers in the dark. She fought the urge to shiver. She refused to give any outward indication of the effect of his nearness on her.

"And the reason I said 'kisses' is because there will be more," he told her.

"That's quite an assumption to make," she said.

"I know."

His lips curved, just a little, before they covered hers.

It was a gentle kiss this time—teasing, testing. As if, despite the previous kiss they'd shared, he was unsure what her response would be this time.

Erin had no doubts. She was sure that she could—*would*—resist.

Her certainty lasted all of about two seconds. Because in the moment that his mouth first brushed against hers, every thought of protest, every ounce of resistance, simply melted away in response to the heat that churned through her body.

The sciences had never been her forte, but she did understand the basics of simple chemistry. And it didn't get much more basic than the rubbing of a man and a woman together resulting in physical attraction.

She knew there were exceptions to the rule. Trevor had been one of those exceptions. However, Corey was the poster boy for the rule. And in his arms, Erin was nothing more than a reactant.

She had no free will, no ability to control her own response where he was concerned, and no desire to be anywhere but in his arms.

Already the feel of his mouth on hers was familiar, his flavor addictive. She'd wanted this—wanted *him*—from the first, and the knowledge shook her. Or maybe it was the kiss that made her tremble.

Chapter Six

She'd said their first kiss never should have happened, and maybe she was right about that. But at this point, Corey thought that attempting to deny the attraction between them would be like closing the barn door after the horse had gotten out. And the desire that raced through his veins reminded him of Lucifer racing across the field, sampling his taste of freedom. Heady and reckless and desperate for more.

He desperately wanted more of Erin.

All of Erin.

He already knew how it would be between them, how she would feel, her naked body beneath his, moving against him, willing and eager. How she would wrap herself around him; how he would sink into her warmth and softness.

He could picture it clearly, and the details were so vivid and real, they made him ache.

But somewhere beneath the passion he tasted on her lips,

there was something else. Just a hint of uncertainty, a touch of wariness. He could make her forget all of her doubts. He could simply keep kissing her, touching her and enticing her to the point that her desire overwhelmed any lingering reluctance. But he knew that they would both have regrets if he did.

No, he wouldn't take her to bed until he was certain that she wanted him as much as he wanted her. So instead of letting his hands roam over her and touch her as he craved, he contented himself with holding her. Even when her arms lifted to link behind his head and her body softened against his, he held his own raging desire in check and continued to kiss her.

Just tasting.

Testing.

Tempting.

Except that he wasn't just tempting Erin, he was tempting himself, too. And because there was a definite limit to how much temptation he could endure, he gently eased away. Slowly. Reluctantly.

Her eyelids fluttered, opened, revealing beautiful blue eyes clouded with confusion.

He brushed his thumb over the curve of her bottom lip, moist and swollen from his kiss, and felt her tremble again. He dropped his hand, realizing he was venturing a little too close to the edge of his limits.

"I'll be seeing you again," he promised.

And then, before he could forget his resolution not to take more than she was ready to give, he turned and walked away.

As Erin closed and locked the door at Corey's back, she was more confused than ever. And considering how confused she was when she arrived in Montana, that was saying something.

She desperately wished she had someone to talk to about her feelings for Corey, but who?

Erika was probably the best friend she had in Thunder Canyon, but she was a newlywed who certainly didn't need to be troubled by her friend's romantic woes, not to mention that she was married to Corey's brother.

Haley was the first friend she'd made in town, but as a waitress, part-time student and volunteer counselor at ROOTS—an organization she'd founded to help troubled teens—Haley had more than enough on her plate. And on top of everything else, she was in the midst of her own romance with Marlon Cates.

Erin was pleased that her closest friends were blissfully in love. She wasn't so pleased that their happiness left her to figure out this situation with Corey on her own.

She really didn't want to get involved with him, but she had a feeling he was right—she was already involved. And now that she knew he was planning to stay in Thunder Canyon, at least for the short term, she would have to figure out how she was going to deal with him.

Sure, she could just continue to ignore the attraction she felt, but her attempts to deny the feelings he stirred inside of her had already proved futile. All he had to do was touch her and all of her resistance melted away. And when he kissed her…well, just the memory of his kisses, the masterful seduction of his mouth on hers, made her sigh.

She'd been attracted to other men before, and she'd had a few relationships in her twenty-five years. She'd also had her heart knocked around a few times, and that wasn't an experience she was eager to repeat. Of course, she'd been younger then and more naive, and she'd learned from her mistakes. She didn't lead with her heart anymore, she didn't believe everything a man told her (and she was especially skeptical of declarations of affection made while naked), and she wasn't ever again going to stay in a relationship with someone because she didn't want to hurt his feelings by telling him that there was no zing in the relationship— which is what had gone so wrong with Trevor.

Of course, lack of zing wasn't a problem with Corey. The problem was too much zing. So much zing, in fact, it was interfering with the normal, rational functioning of her brain.

What she needed to do, if she wanted to ensure that her hormones didn't overrule her head, was establish boundaries—and make sure that the man in question was aware of those boundaries. Because Corey Traub with his dark, bedroom eyes and slow, sexy smile and slower, sexier drawl was a cowboy who had undoubtedly left a trail of broken hearts all across Texas, and she had no intention of being his latest conquest. Even if the thought of being conquered by such a man held a certain undeniable appeal.

Which made her again consider that instead of ignoring the attraction, she should embrace it; instead of establishing boundaries, she should obliterate them. So long as they each knew what they wanted from the other, why shouldn't they enjoy being together?

Maybe it was foolish to think that she could indulge in a casual no-strings affair when she'd never done so before. Or maybe that was just another reason why she should go for it. When she'd made the trip to Thunder Canyon, she'd done so knowing that the journey would bring changes to her life. Meeting Corey had given her another opportunity to make another change.

She'd never known anyone like him—he was larger than life, a man strong enough for a woman to lean on, a man she wanted to be with. He didn't strike her as someone who did anything by half measures, and she knew that if she ever made love with him, it would be a spectacular experience.

What worried her was the possibility that he would seduce not just her body but her heart, and that when he was gone she would be left with only memories of the time they'd spent together and her heart in pieces.

Because he *would* go. She knew that. He had no more intention of staying in Thunder Canyon than she did—but she wasn't ready to pack up her bags just yet.

And although heading back to San Diego held a certain appeal, she knew she couldn't do it. She couldn't go back to her old life and pretend that everything was as it had always been. She'd come to Montana because she needed answers, and she wasn't going anywhere until she had them.

After another restless night, Erin got up Tuesday morning and readied herself for work as if it was any other day. Because her dreams had been mostly centered on Corey, she hadn't come up with any revelations about how to tell her boss about the possibility that he could be her brother. Instead, she decided to act as normal as possible, as if nothing had changed.

But she found herself making excuses to walk past his office, trying to catch a glimpse of him, trying to figure out if there was any familial resemblance between herself and her boss. She had two brothers, and she loved both Jake and Josh, but there was just something about Grant Clifton that had appealed to her from the start.

A man didn't rise to the position he was in without having a fair amount of drive and ambition, but he wasn't ruthless or hard. Her own experience had shown her that he was a fair and compassionate employer; according to his friends, he was loyal and steadfast; the love he obviously shared with his wife of three years proved he was faithful and devoted; and when he talked about his mother and his sister, he demonstrated that he had a strong sense of family.

Was it possible that she might be part of his family? If so, would he grow to care about her as he obviously cared about Elise? Of course, if it turned out that Erin was his sister, it would mean that Elise was not.

How would he deal with that revelation? Would he resent Erin for bringing it to light? Or would he accept that she was as much a victim of circumstances as everyone else?

"Is everything okay?"

Erin realized that she'd been standing in front of the reservation computer for several minutes without inputting any data. She looked up at Carrie and managed to smile. "Sorry. I don't know where my mind is today."

"I think I know," her coworker teased, nodding her head in the direction of the counter.

Glancing past her, Erin saw Corey standing there, and her heart gave that all-too familiar jolt.

"What's he doing here?"

"Looking for you," Carrie told her. "And honey, if you're not interested, feel free to give him my number."

Erin felt her cheeks flush as she moved past her coworker to the counter.

"Are you here to see if I was playing hooky today?" she asked him.

"Nope. Just to see you."

"Any particular reason?"

"You were on my mind. In fact, you've been on my mind since I left your house last night, a detail that did not go unnoticed by my associates at the meetings I had this morning."

She wasn't sure how to respond to that, so she remained silent.

"This is where you could say that you've been thinking about me, too," he prompted.

She didn't think his ego needed the boost of hearing the words, even if they were true. But she folded her arms on the counter and dropped her voice, as if making a confession. "What if I tell you that, as I drove to work this morning, I was thinking about playing hooky again because it's much too beautiful a day to be cooped up inside?"

He leaned closer, so their faces were only inches apart. "Did you think about playing hooky again with me?"

"A girl has to have a few secrets," she teased.

"Something tells me you have more than a few."

It was an effort to keep her smile in place as his words struck a chord. He was right. She had more secrets than anyone in Thunder Canyon knew, more than anyone would possibly guess. And the longer she stayed, continuing to perpetuate the myth that she was just a California transplant looking for a change of pace, the guiltier she felt. She'd made friends with the people in town, listened to their confessions and hopes and dreams.

But she hadn't told a single one of them her real reason for coming to Thunder Canyon. Not even Erika, who had chosen Erin to be the maid of honor at her wedding. And now Erika was married to Dillon, and Erin was fighting her attraction to Dillon's brother, who happened to be good friends with Grant Clifton, who might be Erin's brother. There were too many strings connecting all the players in the drama of her life, and they were getting all tangled up.

She'd been dishonest with so many people. Even if she wasn't guilty of telling lies, she certainly hadn't volunteered the complete truth. And she couldn't help but wonder what they would think of her when they found out. Would the people who had become her friends understand why she'd been silent about her true purpose for coming to Thunder Canyon? Or would the truth cost her those new but treasured friendships?

Her mother tried to instill in all of her kids the importance of being honest. If you tell the truth, she'd pointed out to them, you won't ever forget what you said. Erin understood the importance of the message and she'd tried to live her life accordingly. That had changed when she came to Thunder Canyon.

No, she admitted to herself, it had changed when she'd said that she was quitting her job in San Diego because she felt as if her life had stagnated since graduation and she wanted to explore some other opportunities. Her parents had been supportive—or tried to be. They'd also been hurt by her decision, but not as hurt as she knew they would be if she'd told him she was going to look for a family that Erma had told her was in Montana.

And that one little lie had led to more little lies. Since coming to Thunder Canyon, however, she'd been guilty of so many deceptions and half-truths she wasn't sure she could even remember them all. And she feared that those half-truths were going to come back to haunt her.

Maybe she'd believed they were necessary. Maybe she still did. She couldn't imagine how the tightly knit community would have responded if she'd slapped the newspaper clipping down on a table at The Hitching Post the first day she'd arrived in town and proclaimed that she was related to some or all of the persons in the photo.

Instead, she'd taken a more subtle approach. She'd gotten to know the residents of Thunder Canyon and asked some discreet questions about the families in that faded picture. Unfortunately, the responses she'd received to those inquiries had told her little. And although there was no shortage of skeletons in the closets of the residents of Thunder Canyon, she hadn't heard any murmurs about anyone losing a baby more than twenty-five years earlier.

And then, by sheer luck, she happened to be nearby when Grant Clifton pulled a picture of his sister out of his wallet. Coincidentally, that sister was born on the same day in the same hospital as Erin, and she had some similar features to each of Erin's brothers.

But Erin still didn't know what to do now, how to verify her suspicion that someone at the hospital had somehow mixed up those two babies.

A hand waving in front of her face jolted her out of her reverie. She looked apologetically at Corey. "Sorry."

"Are you sure you don't want to talk about it, darlin'?"

She could hardly deny that her mind had been wandering again, so she only shook her head. "No, I'm not sure. But it's not something I can talk about. Not right now."

"Will you keep me in mind, when you can?"

She wouldn't have blamed him for feeling dissed by her lack of attention, but he seemed more concerned than offended, and she was touched by his offer. "I will," she promised. "Thanks."

"So why don't we talk about your lunch plans?" he said. "Do you have a date with Stefan or can I steal you away for a little while?"

"Why are you so determined to take me to lunch?"

He shrugged. "It's lunchtime, I'm hungry and I enjoy your company."

"How could any woman refuse such a gracious invitation?"

"Stefan was booked, wasn't he?"

"Until four-thirty," she admitted.

"Then he won't be putting his hands on you today," Corey noted.

It was the hint of smugness in his tone that prompted her to tease, "Not until this afternoon."

Erin retrieved her purse from her desk and came around to the other side of the counter.

"How does DJ's Rib Shack sound?" Corey asked her.

"My mouth is watering already," she told him.

He reached for her hand and was pleased when she didn't pull hers away. It was a small thing, but it meant a lot to him because it proved that she was starting to feel comfortable with him.

"But we might have some trouble getting seated," Erin warned. "We have a conference group that booked several large tables for lunch there today."

"Are you forgetting that DJ is my cousin?"

"Does that family connection trump a group of fifty-five paying customers?"

He winced. "Well, I'm sure he can find a couple of chairs for us in the kitchen."

Erin laughed.

He liked to hear her laugh. She seemed so serious most of the time, as if there were heavy issues weighing on her mind. But when she laughed, it was like the sun breaking through on a cloudy day. The soft, sexy sound seemed to burst out of her, and her beautiful blue eyes danced and sparkled.

"For DJ's signature rib sandwich, I would happily sit in the kitchen," she told him.

As it turned out, DJ did manage to find them a small table on the opposite side of the room from the conference guests and with a fabulous view of the resort property. Because they both knew what they wanted to eat, he took their orders so that he could get it into the kitchen before the conference group started clamoring for its food. Corey ordered a beer and Erin, because it was the middle of a work day, requested a soft drink.

"So tell me," Erin said, "how you manage to have so much free time when you're supposed to be in town on business."

"I'm my own boss. When I first started out, I worked more than my share of eighty-hour weeks to ensure my business was successful. Now I have the luxury of being able to pick and choose my jobs and the hours that I'm going to work."

She eyed him over the rim of her glass. "Why did you start your own company instead of going to work at Traub Industries?"

"I did work at Traub Industries, as all of my brothers and my sister did. But, although the experience was memorable and I certainly won't complain about the opportunities the company has afforded me, making a career in the oil business wasn't what I wanted to do with my life."

"So who does run the company?"

"My mother took over at the helm when my dad died, and she's still the CEO. My brother Ethan is the CFO. My stepfather is on the board of directors."

"So it really is a family business."

"I guess it is," he agreed.

She tilted her head. "Are there issues between you and your stepfather?"

"No. Not really."

"Which is it—no? Or not really?"

"Peter's a good guy," Corey said. "And he makes my mom happy. It's pretty amazing to think about the fact that he was willing to marry a woman who was on her own with six kids."

"But—" she prompted.

He didn't say anything.

"But he's not your dad," Erin finished for him.

"No, he's not. I was so young when my dad died that my memories of him are pretty foggy, but it was still hard to accept anyone else trying to take his place. It's only recently that I've realized Peter made his own place—and I'm glad it's with my mom." He shook his head. "But it seems that we're always talking about my family—tell me something about yours."

"The Castros aren't nearly as interesting as the Traubs," she said.

"That's an opinion, not a fact," he chided.

She shrugged. "Okay, my parents are Jack and Betty. My dad's a harbor cop and my mom is a high school history teacher. I have two brothers, Jake and Josh, both of them older. Jake is a cop in New Orleans and Josh is a perpetual student. He's currently studying geosciences at Princeton."

"And what do your parents think of your decision to move to Montana?"

"They're trying to be supportive. They understand that I needed to make some changes in my life. They just wish I didn't have to make them so far away."

"It could be worse," Corey said philosophically. "You could have gone to New England."

She smiled. "Which is what I remind them whenever they start complaining about how far away Thunder Canyon is from San Diego."

"Do you get home to visit them very often?"

"Only once since I moved here," she admitted. "I'd hoped to go back again for Thanksgiving, but that doesn't look like it's going to work out now."

"It's hard being away from family, especially at the holidays."

She nodded. "I don't think I've ever missed a major holiday with them."

"So why don't you invite them to come here?"

She seemed startled by the suggestion. "I can't believe I didn't think of that."

"Sometimes it takes someone from the outside to see the possible solutions to a problem."

"That's exactly what you do, isn't it? Companies hire you to come in and determine what's not working, and you fix it."

"I offer suggestions," he clarified.

"And if a company doesn't take your suggestions?"

"People don't often ignore advice that they pay for, but it's always their choice."

The waiter brought their lunches.

Erin plucked a curly fry from her plate and bit off the end. "How long does it usually take—your review and analysis?"

"Are you trying to figure out how long I'm going to be in Thunder Canyon?" he teased.

"I'm trying to make conversation," she retorted, but the flush in her cheeks confirmed his guess.

"Well, the answer to that question is that it varies depending on the complexity of the problems. Is the company simply looking to improve its bottom line, or is it teetering on the edge of bankruptcy? Is it a mom-and-pop operation or an international conglomerate?" He picked up his spicy barbecue chicken sandwich and bit into it.

"So it could be weeks or months," she guessed.

He nodded, chewing.

"Do you enjoy it?"

"I enjoy the challenge."

"Is that why you're here with me now—because I turned you down the first time you asked me to dance?"

"*You're* here with *me*," he pointed out. "And if you'd accepted my original invitation, the only thing that would have been different is that we would have shared our first dance sooner."

"First dance?"

He grinned. "Yeah, I'm counting on there being more."

She smiled back, not protesting his assumption this time. Then her gaze slid away, caught by something across the room. Glancing over his shoulder, he saw that it wasn't a "something" but "someone"—her boss, Grant Clifton. But it wasn't the direction of her gaze that bothered him so much as the brief glimpse of yearning that he read in her eyes.

Then she focused on her plate again, and Corey was left to wonder if he'd just imagined the longing he thought he'd seen. He hoped so. He sure as heck didn't want to think that she was lusting after a man who was his friend, her boss and married to boot.

However, it would explain why she'd been resistant to his overtures. Not that he thought he was irresistible, but in his experience, most women were flattered by his attention and often sought him out, and he'd been trying to figure out why Erin seemed impervious to his legendary charms.

He'd considered the usual reasons—she was just getting over a failed relationship, she didn't like the color of his hair or his eyes, she thought he was too tall/too short or too young/too old, or she just wasn't attracted to him— although he'd discarded *that* possibility after their first kiss because he knew that a woman couldn't kiss a man the way she'd kissed him if she didn't feel at least some degree of attraction. It had never occurred to him that she might be infatuated with her boss.

"How's your sandwich?" Erin asked.

"Great," he said, and picked it up again.

They chatted casually as they finished their lunches. He noticed that Erin was both attentive and entertaining, her focus never again wavering. Maybe he had imagined the look she'd sent in Grant's direction. Maybe she'd actually been looking at someone else's lunch—or their dessert. He'd dated a lot of women who looked enviously at the cheesecake on someone else's plate but refused to order their own.

"Dessert?" he asked her.

There was still a handful of fries on Erin's plate when she pushed it aside, shaking her head. "I couldn't eat another bite."

"Not even a tiny slice of pecan turtle pie?"

She sighed wistfully. "As much as I love DJ's pecan turtle pie, I know they don't serve tiny slices."

He flagged down their server and ordered a slice anyway, asking for it to be boxed so Erin could take it home.

The cake was delivered along with his credit card slip, and Corey slid the dessert across the table to her.

"I really don't need the three thousand calories in this box," she told him. "But I'll say 'thank you' anyway, knowing that I will savor every last bite while I'm watching *American Idol* tonight."

"What do you watch on Fridays?" Corey asked, as they headed out of the restaurant.

"Nothing in particular."

"Then how about catching a movie with me?" he suggested.

"What movie?" she asked.

"I don't even know what's showing," he admitted.

"I would have expected you to find that out before you decided you wanted to go."

"I just thought it would be fun to go to a movie with you."

"I don't like horror flicks," she warned him.

"You could snuggle up to me during the scary parts." He wiggled his eyebrows suggestively.

She laughed but shook her head. "All the parts are scary parts, and I'd have nightmares for a week."

"Okay, no horror flicks," he promised.

"And I'm not big on sci-fi, either."

He nodded his understanding. "Aliens can be pretty scary."

Her gaze narrowed. "Are you mocking me?"

"Of course not," he said, but his lips twitched as he tried not to smile.

"Just for that, you have to buy the popcorn."

"It would be my pleasure," he told her, and he meant it.

She eyed him warily. "What are we doing, Corey?"

"Setting up a date."

"Is it that simple?"

"For now." They were back at the reception desk, and as much as he wanted to linger, he knew she needed to get back to work. "I'll give you a call to let you know what time on Friday."

"Okay," she agreed. "Thanks for lunch."

As she started around the counter, he caught her hand. She looked up at him, questioning, and he bent his head to touch his lips to hers. It was a quick and easy kiss that was over before she could think to protest about the inappropriateness of him kissing her at work.

"It was my pleasure," he said, and walked away with a smile on his face.

Chapter Seven

He called her on Wednesday, ostensibly to discuss the movie schedule for Friday night. They talked for more than an hour.

They went to the local theater on Friday to see a romantic comedy that Erin had expressed an interest in. Corey grumbled about "chick flicks" throughout the drive back to her condo, but she'd heard him laugh out loud at different parts of the film so she knew he was only teasing.

Because she'd missed work on Monday, she agreed to cover Carrie's shift Saturday morning. She planned to spend the afternoon catching up on the chores she'd neglected during the week—most notably her grocery shopping and housecleaning. But Corey's truck was in her driveway when she got home from the Super Saver Mart, and when he asked her to go horseback riding again, it sounded a lot more fun than scrubbing her shower.

Afterward, they picked up a pizza and a bottle of wine

and took them back to Erin's. As she sat beside him on the couch, watching the flames flicker in the fireplace, she found it hard to believe that she'd only met him a week earlier. So much time seemed to have passed since then.

Sunday morning she awoke to find the snow blowing outside of her windows and decided that the near-blizzard conditions were reason not to venture out of the house. But Corey had no similar qualms because he came over shortly after lunch with some movies he'd rented, and they spent the rest of the afternoon snuggled together on her couch, munching popcorn and watching the original *Star Wars* trilogy. Because, despite her admitted lack of appreciation for the sci-fi genre, he somehow managed to convince her that the George Lucas masterpieces couldn't be so simply classified, and she soon found herself deeply engrossed in the movies.

As the final credits of *The Empire Strikes Back* scrolled on the screen, Erin's stomach began to grumble. Glancing at the glowing numbers on the DVD player, she was surprised to realize how quickly the afternoon had gone and it seemed natural to invite Corey to stay for dinner. Though she hadn't consciously thought about it while she'd been grocery shopping the day before, she'd picked up all the necessary ingredients for her mom's famous enchiladas and Corey seemed pleased by her invitation and happy to eat with her.

After dinner, they tidied up the kitchen together, but when Corey suggested that he should head out, Erin was the one to protest. She wanted to know if Leia succeeded in rescuing Han, to which Corey reminded her that the movie was about a lot more than a romantic subplot. But, of course, he put the third movie on.

It was late by the time he finally said good-night, and several inches of snow had fallen. Erin cringed at the sight of the white stuff covering her car and her driveway, but she decided to ignore it until the morning. Corey wouldn't hear of it though and, after locating a shovel in the garage, insisted on clearing her steps and driveway. Although she appreciated not having to do it herself, she wasn't sure how she felt about his insistence on taking charge.

Not that she was really surprised—she'd instinctively known that he was the type of man who liked to be in control of any situation—but she didn't want him to think that she couldn't take care of herself. She prided herself on her self-sufficiency and independence. She didn't really want to battle with him over clearing snow, but she wanted him to know that she was capable. However, as she watched Corey clear her driveway, effortlessly tossing shovels full of snow aside, she had to admit that there were worse things than having a strong, handsome man around to perform such chores.

When he finished shoveling, she invited him to come back inside for a cup of hot chocolate to warm him up. He declined the drink but did come back inside to kiss her goodbye, and she couldn't deny that the heat they generated between them was—

She jolted as his ice cold hands slipped under her sweater and splayed against the bare skin of her back. Corey laughed and reached for her again, but she stepped away.

The wicked light in his eyes made her heart pound with anticipation; the sexy curve of his lips made her knees weak. She dodged around to the other side of the table, he feinted to the right and caught her when she turned in the opposite direction.

They were both laughing when her cell phone chimed.

Corey frowned. "Who would be calling at this hour?"

"It's a text," she said, reaching for the phone to check the message. "From Grant."

His hands dropped away and he reached for the jacket he'd hung over the back of a chair.

"Carrie called in sick for tomorrow, so he just wanted to give Trina and me the heads-up that we'll be on our own," she explained.

"Didn't you cover for Carrie yesterday?"

She nodded. "She wanted the morning to get ready for a big date." Which made her suspect that her coworker wasn't sick at all but was simply having too much fun with her date to want it to end just yet.

"So she's probably not sick at all," Corey surmised.

Erin just shrugged because she knew she wasn't in any position to judge. Her own reasons for playing hooky the previous week might have been different, but she'd still called in sick when she really wasn't.

"Does that mean you'll have to work later tomorrow?"

"Only if someone on the afternoon shift calls in."

"Or if Grant needs you to fill in somewhere else around the resort," he guessed.

Was that an edge she heard in his voice, or was she imagining it?

"Since I started at the resort, I've never turned down any overtime that was offered because I never had any reason to. But if I have plans, I am allowed to say 'no' to extra shifts," she told him.

"Then you should know that we have plans for tomorrow night."

He was taking charge again, and she wondered if she should protest. But she wanted to see him, so there really wasn't any point. Instead, she asked, "Are you going to tell me what those plans are?"

"As soon as I figure them out," he said, and slid his arms around her waist again. She stiffened, remembering the shock of his icy hands against her skin, but he kept his hands on the outside of her clothes this time. "Right now, I only know that I want to be with you."

"That's good enough for me," she told him, and tugged his head down to hers.

She'd never initiated a kiss before, and she could tell that she'd surprised him by doing so now. He kissed her back, but he let her set the pace, and when she withdrew, he let her go.

As she watched him drive away, she was already anticipating seeing him again, and that worried her—more than a little.

They were spending a lot of time together and people were beginning to talk. Corey didn't seem to care and Erin knew that she shouldn't either, but it bothered her that being seen with him seemed a noteworthy event to the residents of Thunder Canyon. For months, she'd managed to avoid speculation and scrutiny by mostly keeping to herself. And in the space of a week, he'd managed to thrust her into the spotlight.

She could have stopped seeing him. She didn't have to answer his calls, she didn't need to accept his invitations and she certainly wasn't under any obligation to respond to his kisses. But she enjoyed talking to him, she had a good time when they were together, and the passion he stirred inside of her refused to be ignored.

The problem was that spending so much time with Corey meant she didn't have any time to search for the answers she'd come to Thunder Canyon to find. Yet she'd waited almost twenty-six years already, so there wasn't any pressing urgency right now. And because she didn't know how long Corey would be staying in town, she was going to enjoy spending every minute with him that she could.

The following Tuesday afternoon, Corey was feeling bored with his own company so he called Dillon and asked him to come out to the Hitching Post for a beer. He didn't really expect his newlywed brother to accept the invitation, but Dillon—abandoned by his wife and daughter for Holly Clifton's baby shower—said he'd be happy to meet him.

They opted to sit at the bar and within minutes were settled into their seats with frosty glasses of beer in front of them.

"I heard you've been spending a lot of time with Erin Castro," Dillon said.

Corey didn't bother to ask where his brother had heard. In a town the size of Thunder Canyon, rumors spread faster than a bushfire in July.

"I like her," he said simply.

But something in his tone must have given him away because Dillon's gaze narrowed. "You've only known her a week."

A week and a half, actually, but he didn't think the clarification would mean much to his brother. "Sometimes you just know."

Dillon shook his head as he munched on a pretzel.

"I think she might really be the one."

"You think every woman might be the one."

Corey couldn't deny that he'd made the same claim once or twice before. When he was younger, he'd trusted in the basic honesty and goodness of other people—and of women, in particular. As a result, he'd fallen in love readily and frequently. Then he'd met Heather, and he'd learned that people weren't always what they seemed. Although that experience had made him wary, there was something about Erin that urged him to open his heart and trust again, something about her innate sweetness that made him want to believe not just in her but in the way he felt when he was with her. "So I'm an optimist. But this time, it's different.

She's different—she's more real than any woman I've ever known."

"Just…be careful," Dillon cautioned.

He laughed. "You're warning me to be careful of Erin?"

"You don't know her very well," his brother reminded him, casting a pointed glance at the portrait of the town's original "Shady Lady" hanging over the bar. "In fact, no one in Thunder Canyon really knows Erin that well."

Corey didn't like the implication. "Why are you so suspicious? It's not as if entry past the town limits is by invitation only."

"I'm…uncertain…of her reasons for coming to Thunder Canyon," Dillon clarified.

"Maybe she just wanted a change of pace."

"Is that what she told you?"

"As a matter of fact, it is."

Dillon tipped his glass to his lips, drank. "A rather vague response, don't you think?"

He hadn't thought so at the time, but his brother's question had him frowning now. "I think that she'll tell me more when she's ready."

"Whenever that might be."

He picked up his beer. "What's that supposed to mean?"

"Just that she seems to ask a lot of questions without giving away any information about herself," his brother noted.

Corey had noticed the same thing, and he'd admired her ability to draw out other people. It was a valuable skill for someone working in the hospitality industry, and it irked him that his brother was turning it into something negative.

"What have you got against Erin?"

"Nothing," Dillon insisted. "I'm just suggesting that you take your own advice and look before you leap this time."

He took a long swallow from his glass and tried not to wince at the "this time." His brother was right—he had a habit of wanting to believe the best of people, and he'd ended up getting burned because of it. Maybe learning the details of Heather's job hadn't broken his heart, but the truth had dented the hell out of his pride and her lies had destroyed his trust.

But Erin was different. He was sure of it. "Maybe we should talk about something else," he suggested.

"Anything in particular on your mind?"

"The resort."

"What about it?" Dillon wondered.

"It's obvious that the recession has taken its toll on Thunder Canyon, and the resort is no exception."

"You're not telling me anything I don't know," Dillon said.

Corey reached for the bowl of pretzels. "I will," he promised, and proceeded to outline the basic plan he'd worked up to attract new investors and capital to the resort.

Corey had late meetings on Wednesday, so Erin didn't see him again until Thursday when he stopped by the reservation desk to ask her if she wanted to go out for dinner that night. She was conscious of Trina and Carrie watching and growing weary of the talk around town, so instead of accepting his invitation, she offered to cook for him at her place again.

Corey said that he would bring wine and dessert, and he showed up promptly at seven o'clock with a bottle of pinot noir and a bakery box containing two wide slices of DJ's turtle pecan pie.

She'd marinated strips of steak in teriyaki sauce and

stir-fried the meat with red and green peppers, snow peas and carrots, then served it on top of hot basmati rice. It was a favorite recipe of Erin's because it required little time to cook and even less to prep, but Corey obviously enjoyed it as much as she did, as evidenced by the second helping that he finished as readily as the first.

"So why Montana?" Corey asked, tipping the last of the wine into Erin's glass. "What brought you here?"

Their conversation during dinner had mostly touched on inconsequential topics, so his question now seemed to come at her out of the blue. But she'd been regretting all the secrecy and evasions that had been part of any conversations she'd had since coming to town, and she was almost grateful for this chance to tell someone the truth. Or at least part of it.

"I was born in Thunder Canyon," she told him now.

"No kidding?"

"I never actually lived here, but my parents were visiting my great aunt Erma when my mom went into labor ahead of schedule."

"Does your aunt still live here?"

She licked the last bit of caramel from her fork and then pushed aside her empty plate. "She's the one who recently passed away."

"Is that why you came here—to remember her?" he asked gently.

She gathered up their dessert plates and carried them to the counter. She heard the scrape of his chair legs against the tile floor as he pushed away from the table.

"I came here—" she hesitated, still not sure how much to reveal. She needed to confide in someone and she wanted that someone to be Corey, but she really didn't know him well enough to even guess how he might respond. "I came here because it was what she wanted."

"But why did you stay? I mean, a quick visit would have honored her wishes."

She washed and dried her hands before turning back to him. "I stayed partly because I don't yet have the answers I'm looking for and partly because I fell in love with the town the first minute I stepped into the Hitching Post."

"Love can happen like that," he agreed, settling his hands on her hips and pulling her closer. "Hitting you like a ton of bricks when you least expect it."

Corey could tell that Erin didn't know how to interpret his statement never mind respond to it, and he mentally cursed himself for not censoring his words. While he'd realized that the feelings he had for her were stronger and deeper than he'd expected, he shouldn't have assumed that she would feel the same way.

"I guess you're right," she said, looking at the button at his throat rather than at him. "Although I've never really experienced anything like that before."

Which wasn't an admission that she was experiencing anything like that now, but it also wasn't a rejection of his feelings.

"I know we haven't known each other very long—"

"Not even two weeks," she interjected hastily.

"You think I'm rushing things?"

"I think—" she sighed. "I don't know what I think. I have feelings for you—feelings I didn't expect to have. But—"

He could be satisfied with that, at least for now. And not wanting to hear whatever limitations or conditions she was probably going to put on her feelings, he silenced her words with his lips.

Her mouth softened beneath his, her lips parted.

He loved kissing her. She was so warm and passionate, so incredibly responsive. His tongue danced with hers, and his blood surged in his veins. She sighed and shifted closer.

His fingers made quick work of the buttons down the front of her shirt, then his hands slipped inside, cupping soft, round breasts encased in delicate lace. His thumbs stroked over her nipples, and they responded immediately to his touch. He circled the rigid points, felt her tremble.

His lips eased away from hers to trail kisses across her jaw. He touched his tongue to the rapidly beating pulse point at her throat, and she moaned. His mouth moved down her throat, toward the hollow between her breasts, and she shuddered.

He unhooked the clip at the front of her bra and filled his hands with her breasts. Her skin was so soft, so lush, so irresistible. He lowered his mouth to take one turgid peak between his lips. He swirled his tongue around the nipple, then suckled hard. She gasped. Her fingers sifted through his hair, holding him against her, silently urging him to continue.

He was more than happy to comply. He took his time, savoring the flavor of her flesh, learning what she liked by listening to her moans and sighs. As his mouth pleasured her breasts, his hands moved lower. He unfastened the button of her pants, slid down the zipper and dipped inside. Her panties were lace, like her bra, and he could feel her heat and wetness as he stroked her through the fabric. She moaned and arched into his palm, shuddering when he stroked her again.

Then, suddenly, her hands were on his chest, and she was pushing him away.

"No. We have to stop. I can't do this." Though her words were unequivocal, he heard the anguish in her voice and knew that she hadn't really wanted to push him away.

But Corey didn't have any trouble understanding "no" and, although he might regret that the war between desire and conscience had been won by her conscience, he couldn't deny that it had. He thrust his hands into the pockets of his jeans so that he wouldn't be tempted to touch her again, not until he had his own raging desires under control.

He caught a glimpse of tears in her eyes before she dropped her gaze, and he felt like a complete louse. "I'm sorry," he said, and winced at the inadequacy of the words.

Erin shook her head, her fingers trembling as she refastened the buttons on her shirt. "No, *I'm* sorry. I didn't mean to let things go so far. I'm not the type—"

He touched a finger to her lips, halting the flow of words. "You don't have anything to apologize for. I was rushing you," he admitted. "I can't seem to help myself. I want you, Erin. Every time I see you, I want you more."

"I want you, too, Corey, but I'm not ready for this."

He leaned his forehead against hers, frustrated beyond belief but unwilling to push her. He needed her to want him as much as he wanted her, and until then, he would try to be patient. "Then we'll wait until you are," he said simply.

"That might take some time," she warned him. "There's a lot going on in my life right now, personal issues that I'm trying to figure out, that I need to figure out, before I can even think about getting involved."

"We're already involved," he said again.

She sighed. "Only because you're stubborn and persuasive and far too charming for your own good."

He smiled at that. "And you admitted that you have feelings for me, so I'll be satisfied with that for now."

"I do have feelings for you," she acknowledged. "But I'm not sure what to do about them."

"Why do you have to do anything about them? Why can't we just enjoy being together?"

"Because I know you want more than I've given, and I'm not sure I'm ready to give any more."

"Because of Grant?" The question sprang out of his mouth without any forethought, and he immediately regretted the words. He hadn't realized how much he'd been thinking about her relationship with his friend until now, how much he'd worried about her apparent preoccupation with the man who was her boss.

He gauged her expression carefully, watching for a reaction. He hoped that she would be shocked by his question and immediately deny having any feelings for the other man. And he would believe her because he wanted to move forward with their relationship without the unease that prickled at the back of his neck whenever he saw her with Grant.

She sucked in a breath, obviously surprised by the question—or maybe just surprised that he'd voiced it aloud. When she spoke, her response was both weak and unconvincing and made frustration and anger churn in his gut.

"Wh-what does Grant have to do with any of this?"

"Why don't you tell me?"

"Grant is my boss."

"And my friend."

She only nodded.

"And he's married," Corey reminded her, in case she'd conveniently forgotten that fact.

"I've met his wife," she said. "On several occasions."

"They grew up together, here in Thunder Canyon. Their fathers were best friends."

She nodded again. "I've heard the story—about Grant and Stephanie finding their fathers' bodies after the two men were killed by rustlers."

He didn't detect anything but sorrow in her tone, and he wondered if he could be wrong about her feelings for Grant. He wanted to believe he was wrong, but her response to his mention of the other man's name wasn't something he could disregard. She'd been startled—almost acted guilty—and he couldn't shake the instinct that there was more going on than she was willing to admit.

But he knew Grant. He knew how devoted his friend was to Stephanie. And he didn't believe for a minute that the resort manager would ever cheat on his pregnant wife, so the idea that he was having an affair with Erin was patently ridiculous. Not to mention that she could hardly be tearing up the sheets with her boss when she'd spent most of her free time over the past two weeks with Corey.

But his brother's warnings continued to nag at the back of his mind. *You don't know her very well... she seems to ask a lot of questions without revealing any information about herself... look before you leap this time.*

Corey knew it was too late for that. He had already fallen for Erin. He only hoped that he hadn't fallen for a woman who was in love with another man.

After Corey had gone, Erin continued to think about the questions he'd asked. She didn't know why he'd brought Grant into the conversation; she could only assume that he'd picked up on her interest in her boss and misinterpreted it. She wanted to tell Corey the truth, and she wanted to stop tiptoeing around Grant, pretending that she wasn't carrying a huge secret.

Okay, at this point it was still more of a suspicion than a secret—nothing had been proven. And she didn't know what steps to take next, who to talk to, to confirm her suspicions.

Surprisingly, it was a conversation with her mother later that night that gave her an idea.

"The last time I saw Aunt Erma, she reminded me that she used to live in Thunder Canyon."

"That's how you happened to be born there," Betty reminded her.

"Well, I thought that since I'm here now, I might try to find some of her old friends."

"Erma only lived there a few years while she was married to Irwin, her third husband. When he passed away, she moved on."

"But she mentioned a friend who was a nurse, and I got the impression they may have kept in touch."

"Delores Beckett," Betty said.

"You know her?" Erin asked, surprised by her mother's immediate response.

"Of course. She was the nurse in delivery when you were born."

Chapter Eight

Erin's breath caught. "Aunt Erma didn't tell me that."

"She might not have remembered. It was almost twenty-six years ago," her mother reminded her.

But Erin knew that Erma had remembered, and she understood now why her aunt had mentioned the nurse's name.

If Delores Beckett—she scribbled the name down on the message pad beside the phone so she wouldn't forget it again—had been working when Betty Castro had given birth, then she would know what had happened in the maternity ward that day and if there was any chance that two babies had been mixed up.

"Speaking of which," Betty continued, oblivious to the thoughts swirling in her daughter's head, "your dad and I decided that, if you can't come home for Thanksgiving, we're going to have to come to you."

"Really?" Jack had sounded so doubtful when Erin issued the invitation that she hadn't let herself hope they might accept it. Because as much as she was trying to figure out the mystery Aunt Erma had dumped in her lap, she knew that Betty and Jack would always be her parents, and she missed them so much. "You're going to come here?"

"Do you think we'd pass on the opportunity to spend the holiday with our baby girl?"

Erin felt the sting of tears. "Thanks, Mom."

"You mentioned that it's a busy time at the resort," Betty reminded her. "Does that mean we should make a reservation somewhere else?"

"You don't have to make a reservation anywhere—I have plenty of room here at the condo."

She'd rented a basement apartment when she'd first moved out of the Big Sky Motel and she'd been happy in the unit and with the elderly woman who had rented it to her. But after only a few weeks, Erin had been informed by her landlady that her daughter was divorcing her husband and moving home with her two children, so she needed the space for them.

Thankfully, it was right around the same time that Erin had started temping at the resort, and when she'd mentioned to her boss that she was looking for a new apartment, Grant had suggested one of the condos on site. She'd hesitated, knowing that she didn't need as much space as a condo would provide and certain that she couldn't afford such luxurious accommodations. But the economic downturn had lowered the rents and as a resort employee, Erin was entitled to a further reduction.

The condo was completely furnished and the kitchen was fully equipped, which, for a woman who had arrived in town with two suitcases and a few boxes in her trunk, was essential. It had two fireplaces—one in the main floor living room and one in the master bedroom. And whenever she thought about returning to San Diego, she felt a strange tug in the vicinity of her heart.

But it was more than not wanting to move out of the condo—it was that she didn't want to leave Thunder Canyon. There was just something about the town that made her feel as if she'd finally found a place where she belonged.

"Are you sure?" her mother asked now. "We don't want to put you out."

"The condo has three bedrooms and I only sleep in one."

"In that case, we'll be happy to stay with you," Betty said.

"I'm so glad you're coming," Erin said, her throat tight. "I really miss you guys."

"We miss you, too."

She heard the emotion in her mother's response, and when she finally said goodbye and hung up the phone, she wondered—not for the first time—what she was doing in Thunder Canyon. So what if Betty Castro hadn't given birth to her? She and Jack had raised Erin as their daughter, they'd instilled in her the same values and morals as they'd given to their two sons and they'd loved her. Maybe she hadn't always felt as if she belonged, but she'd never had reason to doubt their affection for her.

And now she was digging into the past, and for what? Was uncovering the truth behind Erma's last words really worth tearing all of their lives apart?

Erin was afraid the answer to that question might turn out to be "no." But as she looked down at the name she'd scrawled on her message pad, she knew she couldn't let it go.

* * *

There were only two Becketts in the Thunder Canyon telephone directory. Neither one of them was a "D."

Erin called the number listed for "R & L Beckett" first. After the fifth ring, she waited, expecting her call to connect to an answering machine. But it rang a sixth time, then a seventh. Who, in this day and age, didn't have an answering machine or voice mail?

Aunt Erma, she remembered. Her parents had given her an answering machine one year for Christmas, but Erma had never even taken it out of the box. If she wasn't home, they could call back, she always said. It wasn't hard to believe that a friend of Erma's might have a similar attitude.

She was just about to hang up when the phone was finally picked up on the other end.

"Hello?" It was a man's voice, deep and strong and breathless, as if he'd had to run to answer the call.

"Mr. Beckett?"

"Yes, this is Reginald Beckett," he said cautiously.

"I'm sorry to bother you, but I'm trying to locate a Delores Beckett and I was wondering if she might be a relative of yours."

"No, there isn't anyone in my family by that name."

And that quickly, the hope that had only started to build was knocked down again. She apologized to Mr. Beckett again for bothering him and went to the next listing. This time, her call was picked up on the third ring.

"Yes, hello?" the woman who answered said impatiently.

"I'm looking for Delores Beckett," Erin said.

"Who is this? Why are you looking for Delores?"

"My aunt was a friend of hers, and she suggested that I look up Delores when I was in Thunder Canyon."

"What made you think she would be here?" the woman asked.

"It's not that I thought she would so much as I was hoping that you might be able to help me find her."

"I'm sorry. I can't do that."

She wasn't sure how to interpret that response. The woman who had been on the other end of the line—who never did identify herself—hadn't actually denied knowing Delores or where to find her.

As Erin listened to the dial tone buzzing in her ear, she noted the address beside the number and thought that maybe she would stop by to chat with Ms. T. Beckett in person.

Hollyhock Lane was located in a newer survey where all of the streets had picturesque-sounding names and postage stamp-sized lots. Number thirty-four was the center unit of a townhouse complex. Erin had driven past the stone-and-brick two-story on her way home from work the day before, but there had been no vehicle in the driveway and no indication that anyone was at home.

On Tuesday she ended up working late so the sun was already down by the time she left the resort. Considering that T. Beckett had been less than warm on the phone, she had no intention of approaching the woman's door in the dark.

But because she finished early on Wednesday if she was scheduled to work on Saturday morning, as she was this week, she was back on Hollyhock Lane by three o'clock that afternoon. She pulled up across the street, trying to get up the nerve to leave her vehicle and approach the door, when a little red Toyota pulled into the driveway.

Well, at least she knew someone was home.

But when the driver got out of her car, Erin realized there was no way she could be Delores Beckett. The woman was barely older than Erin herself. And then she opened the back door and a child—a little girl probably not more than three or four years old—climbed out. They went around to the trunk, and the mother lifted out several grocery bags, handing the lightest one to her daughter before juggling the rest of them along with her purse and keys as they made their way to the door.

With a resigned sigh, Erin pulled away from the curb and drove home.

Maybe Delores Beckett had left town just as Erma had done, moving away to make a new start somewhere else.

But if that was the case, where was Erin supposed to start looking for her?

As Erin was getting ready to leave work the next day, she overheard Grant mention to the afternoon desk manager that he would be at DJ's if there were any problems. She'd been distracted all day, trying to figure out a way to approach him. She had no intention of blurting out that she thought he might be her brother—she just wanted to have a conversation and possibly learn something more about his mother or his sister.

So when she'd finished assigning rooms for the last reservation that had come in through the website, she picked up her purse and headed to DJ's.

She watched the hostess lead Grant to the far side of the room. Her heart was pounding and her hands felt clammy, so she ducked into the restroom, needing a moment to shore up her courage. It was silly, she knew, to be so nervous when she talked to the man every day at work. But those were always work-related discussions and inevitably brief.

She washed her hands, ran a brush through her hair, dabbed on some lip gloss. Then she drew in another breath, pressed a hand to her still-pounding heart and prepared to go talk to the man who might be her brother.

Though she hadn't spoken the words aloud, they seemed to bounce off of the tiled walls and echo in her head.

…might be her brother…her brother…brother…

She nearly jolted when the door opened and another patron entered. Deciding that she'd stalled long enough, she exited into the foyer, hesitating in the entranceway that separated the restrooms from the main part of the restaurant to peek through the brass potted plants that flanked the arch.

She spotted Grant easily. He was sitting so that his profile was to her at a small booth with a curved leather seating area, a half-finished pint of beer on the glossy wooden table in front of him.

She smoothed her hands down the front of her skirt, drew in a deep breath and started toward his table. As she stepped out from behind the plants, she saw him rise to his feet.

She faltered. Had she dallied too long? Was he leaving already?

But he stayed standing where he was, his gaze focused across the room, smiling. And then Stephanie stepped into view. She crossed to her husband and leaned up to kiss him. His arm came around her, pulling her closer, prolonging the kiss.

And Erin knew that her moment had come and gone. It had been one thing to approach Grant when he was alone, and it was quite another to interrupt a private moment with his wife.

She turned away, tears of regret and frustration blurring her eyes and almost walked right into someone.

"Excuse me," she said softly. She stepped aside without looking up, then gasped when she felt a hand on her arm.

"What is going on with you?" Corey demanded.

She tugged her arm out of his grasp. "I don't know what you mean."

"I mean that I want to know why you're lurking in doorways, spying on another man…and his wife."

She didn't know how he knew she'd been watching Grant—unless he'd been watching her. But she didn't think challenging him on that point would do anything to erase the fury she read in his dark eyes. "It's not what you think," she said instead.

"Then what is it?"

She owed him an explanation, but she could hardly tell him what she hadn't been able to tell Grant, so she didn't say anything.

Corey shook his head. "I don't know which one of us is more screwed up—you, for lusting after your boss, or me, for wanting you anyway."

The accusation that she was lusting after Grant was so outrageous—and more than a little disturbing, considering what she suspected about her relationship to the man—that she chose to ignore rather than respond to it.

"I told you there was too much going on in my life to get involved in a personal relationship right now," she reminded him.

"You didn't tell me that what was going on was an infatuation with a married man."

She bit her tongue as another customer approached. When the door to the men's room had closed behind him, she finally said, "I'm not infatuated with Grant."

"Then why are you stalking him?"

His voice had risen, and she looked around, all too aware of their public surroundings. So far, no one seemed to be paying any attention to them, but the last thing she wanted was to draw attention to herself—at least not anymore than she already had.

"I'm not stalking him," she kept her voice quiet but firm. "And I'm not going to continue this ridiculous argument with you here."

She turned and walked away, choosing not the most direct route to the exit but the one that would ensure she didn't have to walk past Grant and Stephanie's table.

Corey followed her, and when they were outside of the restaurant, he stepped in front of her, blocking her path.

"Okay," he said. "If you don't want to continue this argument here, where do you want to continue it?"

"I don't want to continue it at all," she said, and brushed past him.

Corey's fingers closed around her wrist. "We're going to continue it because I want some damn answers about what's going on with you."

She tried to yank her hand out of his grasp, but his hold only tightened. "I don't know if this is how you treat women in Texas, but I don't appreciate being manhandled."

"You didn't object to my hands being on you the other day," he reminded her. "Or were you pretending that it was Grant who was touching you?"

"No," she denied, shocked that he would even suggest such a thing.

"So what is it, Erin?"

She swallowed, suddenly aware of the dangerous glint in his eye, the banked heat in their depths. "If you want to continue this conversation, we can go to my place."

"Fine. We'll take my truck."

"I have my own—"

"We'll take mine," he insisted.

Erin knew she should be annoyed with him, both with his high-handed attitude and his demands for answers. But as he led the way to his truck, she felt her annoyance fading. Looking at the situation from his perspective—seeing what he'd seen, thinking of her continued evasions—she could understand why he'd have questions.

She had to hurry to keep pace with him because his fingers were still firmly clamped around her wrist, but he wasn't hurting her. She also knew he *wouldn't* hurt her. Not physically, anyway.

He was a man who was used to taking charge and accustomed to getting what he wanted. But the other night, when he'd had her so aroused she'd almost begged him to make love with her, it had only taken a single word to have him backing off.

He helped her into the truck, then went around to the driver's side. Neither of them said anything during the short drive to her condo, leaving Erin with no escape from her own thoughts. And those thoughts kept taking her back to the intimate encounter in her kitchen.

He must have known that he could have changed her mind. Another kiss, a single touch, and she would have been putty in his hands. But he'd respected her need to put a halt to things; he'd accepted that she wasn't ready.

She was ready now.

She was shocked to realize it was true, but she was unable to deny it. She wanted him. Maybe it was the realization that she would be in control, that this incredibly strong and sexy man would accede to her wishes, pleasure her as she wanted—

Corey killed the engine. As they approached her front door, Erin drew a deep breath and reached for the door handle. Her fingers fumbled with her keys, but she finally managed to locate the right one and insert it in the lock. She was all too aware of Corey standing right behind her, so close that she could feel the heat from his body, and her knees trembled.

She set her purse and keys on the table, then stripped off her coat and hung it carefully on a hanger in the closet. Corey shrugged out of his leather jacket and tossed it over the arm of the sofa. When she turned to face him, he was standing with his arms folded across his chest, watching her. He was still angry, she could see it in his eyes. But there was something else there, a glint that hinted at the same heat that was churning through her own veins.

Her heart was pounding, her throat was dry. She had to lick her lips to moisten them before she could talk, and she noticed that his gaze zeroed in on the movement, and his already dark eyes grew darker.

"You said you wanted answers," she reminded him.

"Answers are the least of what I want, darlin', but that's probably a good place to start."

"Are you going to come in? Or did you want to finish this standing in the hall?" She started toward the kitchen. "I could put on a pot of coffee."

"Don't."

She halted in mid-step. "You don't want coffee."

"I don't want to have this conversation in the kitchen."

And suddenly she knew why—because he was thinking of the last time they'd been in her kitchen together, when she'd been half-naked and whimpering in his arms.

"Okay." She swallowed and pivoted toward the living room. "No coffee."

She needed to tell him about Grant, she wanted him to understand the true nature of her interest in her boss, but first she felt compelled to respond to the accusations he'd made outside of the restaurant.

"Before I explain about Grant, you need to understand that you were way off base when you accused me of having any kind of romantic interest in him. I was shocked and offended by the suggestion that I could be thinking of him while I was with you, but then I realized you don't really know me any more than I know you, and it's important to me that you believe I could never be with one man if I wanted another."

He took a step toward her. "So you were thinking of me, when I was kissing you and touching you and—"

"Yes," she admitted. "I was thinking of you."

"And you were wanting me?" he prompted.

She swallowed. "Corey—"

He touched his fingers to her lips, halting her protest. He traced the shape of her mouth. His touch was gentle now, infinitely seductive. And that quickly the mood changed.

The anger that had snapped and crackled in the air between them was something different now. But somehow the desire she saw was even more dangerous than the anger because she knew that her own desire was just as powerful, and that neither would be denied this time.

His fingertips skimmed over her cheek, traced the outline of her ear, making her shiver. "Corey, please, I need to explain—"

"I don't want to argue about this anymore," he told her.

His fingertips slid down her throat, over the curve of her breast. Her breath caught, her legs went weak.

"Corey."

He dipped his head to brush his lips against hers. "Tell me what you want, Erin. If you tell me to go, I'll go. But if that's truly what you want, you better say it loud and fast because what I'm seeing in your eyes is something very different."

"I don't want you to go," she said.

"Then what do you want?"

"You," she said, and lifted her arms to link them around his neck, drawing his head down so that she could kiss him. Long and slow and deep. "I want you."

He pulled her tight against him, proving that he wanted her, too. "Should we go upstairs?"

She shook her head. "I want you here. Now."

"Sounds good to me," he agreed.

But he took a moment to set the scene. He found the remote and started the fire, then he removed the blanket from the back of the sofa and spread it on the floor by the hearth.

"Should I get a bottle of wine?"

"Later," he said, and reached for her again.

He kissed her, gently at first, as if wanting to ensure that this was really what she wanted. She could hardly blame him for his doubts. Only a few days earlier, she'd told him she wasn't ready—but that wasn't entirely true. Even then she'd wanted him, more than she'd ever wanted any other man, but the intensity of those feelings had scared her.

She was still scared. She wasn't the type of woman who gave herself easily to a man. In fact, she'd only ever had two lovers, and both had been men that she'd believed herself in love with, men that—at the time—she'd believed she was building a future with. She had no such illusions about Corey, but she could no longer deny the inevitable. The attraction between them had been escalating to this point since their first meeting.

He nibbled on her bottom lip, tugging with his teeth, teasing with his tongue. His kiss was hot and demanding now, and when his tongue stroked the ultra-sensitive skin on the roof of her mouth, sparks shot through her body and her knees nearly buckled.

She yanked his shirt out of his pants, her fingers fumbling just a little as they made quick work of the buttons that ran down the front. Then her hands were on his skin—hot and smooth—tracing the hard ridges of muscle. The man had the kind of body she'd only ever fantasized about.

She could have spent hours admiring those rippling muscles, exploring all that taut golden skin. But he was still half-dressed and she was suddenly desperate to see all of him. To touch and taste every inch of him.

He was so strong and hard—so undeniably male—and everything that was female inside of her responded to his nearness. When he walked into a room, she could barely tear her eyes away. Now she had him in *her* living room, and she wasn't even going to attempt to keep her hands off of him.

She wasn't usually impulsive or reckless, and she knew that getting naked with a man she hardly knew—a man who obviously had questions and doubts about her—was both impulsive and reckless, but she couldn't continue to deny what they both wanted. What they needed.

Though she hadn't even been aware of him unfastening her skirt, she felt it drop away, pooling at her feet. Her blouse was dispensed with as quickly, leaving her clad in only her bra and panties and stockings. His hands curved over her buttocks, his fingertips skimming down the backs of her thighs before they encountered the lace band at the top of her stockings.

He pulled back, holding her at arms' length to look at her. His eyes glittered in the light of the fire, but it was the heat in their fathomless depths that stoked the flames burning inside of her.

"Do you have any idea how much I want you?" he asked, his voice hoarse with desire.

"Hopefully as much as I want you," she told him and reached for the button at the front of his jeans. She struggled a little with the zipper that was straining over his erection, but when she managed to slide it down and slip her hand inside, she almost moaned with pleasure. Even through the cotton barrier of his briefs, she could tell that he was rock hard and huge, and the discovery made her knees weak.

She slid her hand down the length of him, felt him respond to her caress. A low growl reverberated in his throat and he scooped her off of her feet.

Her heart fluttered inside her breast, though she knew his action wasn't a romantic one so much as a purposeful one. He was the type of man who was used to taking what he wanted, and right now he wanted her.

He lowered her onto the blanket, then straddled her hips with his knees. The gaze that raked over her was hot and hungry and as intimate as a caress. Her whole body ached for him, but now that he had her mostly naked and horizontal, he didn't seem to be in any hurry.

When he did touch her, it was only to push the thin, pink straps of her bra off of her shoulders. Then he lowered his head and nibbled gently along the ridge of her collarbone.

She enjoyed foreplay. Although her experience with sex was admittedly limited, she'd usually found the "before" parts more pleasurable than the "during." But now, with Corey, she wanted nothing so much as she wanted him inside of her.

"Corey."

He lifted his head, and the glint of amusement in his eyes told her that he'd heard the plea in her voice, that he knew exactly what she wanted. And the slow, sexy curve of his lips warned that he was going to enjoy torturing her a little bit more.

"I thought about what you said, darlin'," he told her. "About rushing things. And I've decided that I don't want to rush anything now."

"At this point, I wouldn't object to rushing things a little."

He chuckled softly, then brushed his lips against hers. "Relax."

Relax? How the heck was she supposed to relax when every nerve ending in her body was aching with wanting?

But she let her head fall back and her eyes drift shut.

His fingertips skimmed the curve of her breasts, then dipped into the hollow between them. He unhooked the clasp, then stripped the bra away. Her nipples immediately pebbled, begging for his attention. He didn't disappoint. He bent his head to one breast, taking the rigid peak in his mouth and suckling deeply. The other he palmed, rolling the nipple between his thumb and finger. Sparks of white, hot pleasure shot through her, seeming to bombard her from every direction, arrowing toward her core.

His mouth moved from one breast to the other, laving and suckling and teasing her right to the edge of ecstasy… only to leave her dangling.

With a wicked smile, he abandoned her breasts and took his exploration lower. His mouth left a trail of hot, wet kisses as he made his way down her belly. He hooked his thumbs in the sides of her panties, slowly drew them down her legs, tossed them aside.

"These are nice," he said, his tone almost casual as he stroked his fingertips lightly up the length of her stockings, from her ankles to the inside of her knees to the bands at the top. He traced the lacy edging, slowly, his gentle touch making her shiver.

"Very nice," he amended. "But I think your bare skin will feel even nicer."

She couldn't speak. He had her so completely and desperately aroused she was speechless…and very close to whimpering.

He took his time removing the stockings. He bent one leg at the knee, then traced the lace border again, all the way around this time. Then he slowly rolled down the band, just to her knee, then his fingertips drifted upward again, a feather-light touch against her bare skin. She bit down on her lip to keep from moaning aloud. He lowered his head and kissed the inside of her thigh, then kissed his way down to the sensitive spot at the back of her knee. He rolled the stocking down to her ankle, following the path of the silk with more hot kisses. Then he repeated the same routine with the other stocking, treating her other leg to the same close, personal attention until she was quivering and aching and ready to beg.

His hands stroked over her, from her shoulders to her breasts to her hips, and she trembled everywhere that he touched.

"Corey—please."

He drew away from her only long enough to strip away the last of his clothes and put on protection, and when he lowered himself over her again, she sighed and thought, *Now—finally now.*

Corey had pictured her like this, wanted her like this. Her eyes were glazed, her skin was hot, and she was breathless and trembling, as desperate for him as he was for her.

He could take her now—he could plunge into the slick, wet heat between her thighs and give them both the release they craved. He wanted to take her now, to finally ease the ache that had been building inside of him for weeks, an ache that only she could lessen. But he was determined to give her more. To give her more pleasure than anyone else had ever given her, to be more than anyone had ever been to her.

He knelt between her legs, and she sighed. His hands stroked the soft skin of her inner thighs, and her knees fell open a little farther, silently encouraging his exploration. His thumb stroked over her nub, and she shuddered. He slipped one finger, then two, inside of her, the slick wetness confirming that she was ready for him—more than ready. His erection throbbed painfully, urging him to take what she was offering.

Instead, he curled his hands around her bottom, lifting her hips off the blanket, and lowered his head to take her with his mouth.

She gasped and arched, as if to pull away, but he held her fast and feasted. She tasted as he'd imagined—sweet and seductive—and he savored her feminine flavor. Her shallow, breathless pants assured him that she'd stopped fighting and had surrendered to the pleasure. With his lips and his tongue, he teased her back to the edge where he'd left her teetering so precariously before, but this time, he pushed her not just to the limit but beyond.

He'd known she was a passionate woman. The kisses they'd shared had proved that. What he hadn't known was how incredibly arousing it would be to watch her finally succumb to the passion that burned so hot and bright between them.

He saw her eyes glaze, heard her breath quicken then catch and finally release on a sob. She bucked…shuddered… shattered. Then sank bonelessly back onto the blanket, her eyes closed, her cheeks flushed.

He made his way slowly back up her body, stroking and kissing her until she was trembling again. He kissed her belly, her breasts, her throat. She pulled him up, seeking his mouth with her own, kissing him with the same frenetic passion that was raging inside of him, using her lips and tongue and teeth to drive him as wild as he was driving her.

His body pressed down on hers, his erection nudging at her slick, wet center. She arched her hips, rocking against him. The rhythmic friction was nearly enough to send him over the edge. He scrambled to hold on to the last fraying threads of his self-control with a slippery fist.

"Tell me you want me," he demanded.

"I want you."

"Say my name." He needed to hear his name on her lips, to know that she had no illusions about who she was with.

Her hands slid up his arms, over his shoulders, her fingernails biting into his muscles. "I want you, Corey." She tugged on his bottom lip with her teeth, and he felt the ache spread through him. "Only you."

He'd fantasized about this moment, about the texture of her skin beneath his hands, the taste of her damp, quivering flesh, the sounds she would make as he pleasured her. Even his most explicit fantasies paled in comparison to the reality.

Unable to hold back even a single moment longer, he yanked her hips high and thrust into her. She gasped and arched, pulling him deeper, her muscles clamping around him as she climaxed again. Perspiration beaded his brow as he battled against the pulsing waves that washed over her and threatened to drag him along in their wake. He clenched his teeth as he fought the tide, his fists clutching handfuls of blanket as he rode out her release.

She was gasping and shuddering as he plunged into her, again and again, deeper, harder, faster, and she matched him stroke for stroke. Her nails scored his back, but he didn't feel the pain. He wasn't aware of anything but the desperate urge to take, to claim, to possess.

He fought the haze that blurred his vision, needing to see her, to watch her surrender to the sweet pleasure of their mating. And he swallowed the cries of pleasure that spilled from her lips as another climax pulsed through her and finally dragged him over the edge and into oblivion with her.

Chapter Nine

Erin had always believed that sex was a generally enjoyable if highly overrated experience. Of course, that had been her opinion *before* she had sex with Corey Traub.

After she was seeing things differently.

Or maybe she was still seeing stars.

Later she might worry that there were still secrets between them, but she wouldn't—couldn't—regret making love with him.

Corey had slipped away to deal with the protection, but he'd returned almost immediately and snuggled up with her again.

The flickering flames of the fire cast golden shadows on his face, emphasizing the strong planes and sharp angles. Just looking at him nearly made her sigh again. All those hard, taut muscles, all that smooth, bronzed skin. How was it possible to look at him and not want him?

He was probably too rugged to be considered beautiful,

but in that moment, she thought he was truly the most beautiful man she'd ever known. Certainly he was the most considerate and thorough lover. And though her body had been completely and unquestionably sated, when he stroked a hand down her arm, she felt her blood start to heat again.

"What are you thinking?" he asked.

Her lips curved. "That I was wrong."

He propped himself up on an elbow. "About?"

"Sex."

"How were you wrong?"

His hand had slid from her hip to her breast, his thumb tracing lazy circles around her nipple. An already tight and aching nipple.

"I always thought that the anticipation was so much more exciting than the main event," she admitted.

"And now?" he prompted, nuzzling her throat.

"Now—" she sighed contentedly "—I don't."

His mouth came down on hers, as gentle as a whisper. Not possessing but coaxing, not demanding but giving. And the more he gave, the more she wanted.

She lifted her arms, drew him down to her.

He pressed her back down onto the blanket, then abruptly drew away.

"You know what? I'm starving."

She blinked, stunned by his sudden withdrawal. "I could maybe throw something together," she offered. "But I was supposed to stop and get groceries on my way home, so the fridge is pretty bare."

"Why don't we order something and I'll go pick it up?" He was already reaching for his pants, starting to dress.

"That sounds better than cooking, but why don't we order something and have it delivered?"

"I don't mind going out."

She tugged the blanket up to cover her nakedness. He'd

been so wonderful and attentive earlier that she hadn't felt the least bit self-conscious. But now it seemed that he couldn't get away from her fast enough, and that made her wonder what she'd done wrong.

"So what do you want—Chinese? Pizza? Pasta?"

"I want to know why you're so anxious to get out of here."

He paused with one arm in his shirt. "What?"

She tucked her knees up beneath her chin and stared at the fire. "If you're done with me, just say it. Don't make up excuses to race out the door."

He was immediately beside her, squatting down so that they were at eye level. He touched his hand gently to her cheek. "I'm sorry, darlin'. It never occurred to me that you would think I was running out on you."

"Isn't that exactly what you're doing?"

"No," he denied and brushed his lips against hers. "I only wanted to make a trip to the pharmacy without admitting where I was going."

She drew back. "The pharmacy?"

His smile was wry. "Well, I didn't actually plan for this to happen tonight and we've already used my emergency condom."

"Oh." She felt her cheeks flush. "Well, I didn't plan for this to happen tonight, either, but I thought I should be prepared for…eventually."

"You have protection?"

"A whole box. Upstairs."

He tugged the dangling shirt off his arm, tossed it aside, then scooped her into his arms, blanket and all. "Then I guess we should be upstairs."

"I thought you wanted food."

He was already halfway to her bedroom. "We'll have something delivered."

* * *

Later, they ordered Chinese and opened a bottle of wine. They ate fried rice, Cantonese chow mein and lemon chicken and washed it all down with a light, crisp Chardonnay. Then they made love again.

Corey didn't know what it was about Erin that had gotten so completely under his skin, but no matter how many times he had her, he couldn't seem to get enough. But his feelings for her went much deeper than physical attraction, and there was still so much that he didn't know about her.

He needed to know what was going on, why she seemed so preoccupied with the man who was his friend and her boss. He no longer believed that she was infatuated with Grant. He knew she wouldn't have made love with him as willingly and passionately as she had if she had feelings for another man, but there was definitely something that she wasn't telling him.

He wanted answers, but as connected as he felt to her right now, he wasn't ready to let anything come between them.

They were in her bed, snuggled together beneath the covers. The only light in the room was from the flames of the fire, but he didn't need to see. He'd memorized every detail of her face, every curve of her body.

He lifted a hand to brush a strand of hair off of her cheek. Her lips curved, though her eyes remained closed. "Tired?"

"Exhausted," she admitted.

"Do you have to work tomorrow?"

She shook her head. "No. Although I will have to go pick up my car."

"I'll take you in the morning."

Her eyes flickered open. "You're going to stay?"

"If that's okay."

"That's definitely okay."

"Are you going to make me breakfast?"

"If you consider coffee and toast 'breakfast.'"

"You have to get groceries," he remembered.

She nodded, her eyes drifting shut again.

"Erin—"

He wanted to apologize for the way he'd confronted her at the resort, for what his brothers would undoubtedly refer to as typical high-handed behavior. But he was afraid that mentioning what had happened earlier would lead into a discussion about Grant and after everything they'd shared tonight, he wasn't sure he was ready to have that conversation.

"Mmm," she said.

He brushed his lips to hers. "Sweet dreams."

After the intense physical workout of the night before, Erin suspected that Corey would have preferred a hearty breakfast of eggs and bacon and fried potatoes, but he didn't complain when he got only the toast and coffee she'd promised. In fact, he even helped prepare the simple morning meal.

While Erin set coffee brewing and put the bread in the toaster, Corey embarked on a search through her cupboards for peanut butter and jam. While she buttered the toast, he filled two mugs with coffee and carried them to the table. When they finally sat down together, she noticed that he went for the peanut butter but she preferred jam, that he drank his coffee black while she added lots of milk and sugar to hers.

It was funny, she thought, the things you could learn about a man when you woke up with him in the morning. She'd rarely had that experience before. Though she was almost twenty-six years old, she'd still lived with her parents, and Betty and Jack Castro were not the type to casually accept their daughter spending the night at a man's house.

She'd had a boyfriend from out of town visit her in San Diego for a weekend once. They'd started dating while he'd attended USD and had stayed together after he'd graduated, but it had been difficult to sustain a relationship over the long distance and when he had visited, her parents had put him in her brother Jake's room and made sure they kept their own door—located directly across the hall from their twenty-two-year-old daughter's—open throughout the night.

Of course, Corey had probably slept with a lot of women, and, although she didn't intend to dwell on that thought, the realization did make her feel more than a little awkward. Especially in the morning, when she woke up with her hair in tangles and her face bare of makeup. She didn't know if he sensed her self-consciousness, but he eliminated all traces of it by making love with her again.

It was certainly an effective way to get her blood flowing in the morning, but even as she'd snuggled again in the warm comfort of his arms, she'd been all too aware that things could change in a minute—the minute she told Corey the truth about her reasons for coming to Thunder Canyon.

He hadn't pressed her for an explanation, but she knew he hadn't forgotten their aborted conversation of the day before. More likely, he was giving her an opportunity to explain, as she wanted to do. But she was hesitant to say anything that might jeopardize the comfortable rapport they'd established.

So she was silent about it while they tidied up the kitchen, after which Corey took her to the supermarket to do her grocery shopping. Erin assured him that she could shop on her own—if he would just take her to get her vehicle—but he insisted that he wanted to spend the time with her, and because Erin wanted to be with him, too, she didn't protest too much.

After they'd finished shopping, he took her home again and helped her put away the groceries. It was a routine chore, and one that she'd performed dozens of times by herself. But somehow, with Corey, it was cozy and domestic and it was all too easy to imagine that it could become *their* Saturday morning routine.

Dangerous territory.

She knew that physical intimacy didn't necessarily imply a committed relationship, and she wasn't looking for any long-term promises. She hadn't been looking to get involved at all. But being with Corey had decimated all of her reservations. Being with Corey allowed her to forget that the unanswered questions about her past made it difficult for her to plan a future. Being with Corey made her forget everything except how very much she wanted to be with him.

She tried to play it cool. She didn't want him to know that she'd already given him a very big piece of her heart. Despite the reference he'd made to his feelings for her, she knew that those feelings might change when he learned the truth about her reasons for being in Thunder Canyon. As she'd gotten to know him better, one of the things she'd learned about him was that he was loyal to his family and friends, and she suspected that his uneasiness in believing she had a crush on her boss originated more from his friendship with Grant and Stephanie than any personal jealousy.

It was the issue they'd been ignoring, pretending it didn't exist. But they couldn't continue pretending.

"Looks like it would be a nice day to go riding," Corey said.

Erin looked out the window, at the big, fat flakes of snow that had started to fall. "It's snowing."

"The horses love the snow—it makes them frisky."

"I *don't* love the snow," she told him.

"California girl," he teased.

"Yep."

He chuckled. "Okay, so what do you want to do?"

"Stay indoors where it's warm."

"By the fire?" he prompted huskily.

Her blood heated with the memory of what they'd done by the fire the night before…and in her bedroom…and in the shower.

Yeah, she could think of a lot of ways to pass the time inside with Corey. But first, they had to talk.

"I need to tell you about Grant," she said.

The teasing light faded from his eyes; the muscle in his jaw flexed.

"I'm listening," he said, but the coolness in his tone warned her that he'd started to withdraw already.

"I think—" she drew in a deep breath, blew it out "—I think that Grant Clifton might be my brother."

She knew he'd be surprised, probably even skeptical, but she hadn't expected that he would laugh in response to her statement.

But after a minute of stunned silence, he did just that. "You've got to be kidding. That's why you're so interested in your boss—because you think you're related?"

"I know it sounds unbelievable—"

"Sounds? Darlin', my family has known Grant's family forever, and I can assure you that he only has one sister. What on earth would ever have given you such an outrageous idea?"

She couldn't help but feel irritated by his immediate dismissal of her suggestion. "For starters, Elise Clifton and I share the same birthday."

"Lots of people share their birthdays with other people," he pointed out.

"I was born in Thunder Canyon."

"Again, nothing more than a coincidence," he insisted.

"And Elise looks a lot like each of my brothers," she continued, determined to make her case.

His brows rose. "What are you saying—that you and Elise were switched at birth?"

"It could have happened."

"Maybe—if this was a Sunday afternoon movie."

"Life is often stranger than fiction," she pointed out.

"And what possible motive would someone have for mixing up babies?"

"I'm not suggesting that it was a deliberate switch but an accident."

"Yeah, because that's much more likely," he said drily.

She reminded herself that his skepticism was expected, but it was his obvious disbelief that hurt. She tried to understand—she knew her explanation had surprised him—but she couldn't comprehend how a man who claimed to care about her could so completely disregard something that was so important to her.

"The last time I visited my great aunt Erma, she told me that my real family was in Thunder Canyon."

"And you told me that she was dying when you saw her." His tone was gentle now, sympathetic. "She was probably pumped up on medication and didn't have any idea what she was saying. You can't take someone's delusional ramblings and run with them."

"She was dying but she wasn't delusional," Erin insisted.

"She just wanted to be sure that I knew the truth about my family."

"Did she actually tell you that you and Elise Clifton were switched at birth?"

"No," she admitted, some of her conviction fading, "but—"

"And what does your family think of these claims?" he challenged.

She dropped her gaze, sighed. "I haven't told them."

"Why not?"

"Because I didn't want to upset them until I had proof," she admitted. And maybe because she knew they would be just as skeptical as Corey.

"But you're willing to upset Grant and his sister and their mother?"

"I don't want to upset anyone. I only wanted to talk to Grant, to find out more about his family."

"Is that why you've been asking questions around town? Do you think there was some kind of conspiracy? That the whole town was somehow involved in covering up a baby switch?"

"Of course not," she denied, wondering how he'd managed to twist her words around so completely, and wondering why his obvious lack of faith in her hurt so much.

"Well, if you think you can make that kind of claim and not upset a whole lot of people, you're sorely mistaken, darlin'."

"I just want to know the truth," Erin insisted. "All my life, I've never really belonged—it's like I'm an outsider in my own family."

"Lots of people feel disconnected, but they don't go looking for a new family to replace the one they've got."

"I'm not looking to replace my family. I love my parents and my brothers—"

"If you truly love your parents and your brothers, you'll let this go," he said.

"I can't. I need to find the truth."

"What if the truth is that you are their biological child?"

"What if I'm not?" she countered. "What if Elise Clifton is?"

"What will that change? Even if you're right, what do you hope to accomplish? Do you think anyone will thank you for digging this up?"

Probably not, she admitted to herself. And while the absolute last thing she wanted was to hurt anyone, she knew that continuing to live a lie would hurt, too. Why couldn't he see that she needed to know the truth—that she couldn't begin to move forward until she'd answered the questions about her past?

"Obviously we have a difference of opinion on this."

"I won't help you cause heartache for people I care about. You need to decide what really matters to you—our relationship or this wild goose chase you've set yourself on."

There was something in his tone that was so determined, so final. Was it possible that this was the same man she'd spent the night with? The man she'd not only made love with but realized she was falling in love with? "What are you saying?"

"I'm asking you to forget about this…to just let it go."

She didn't understand why he was so adamant, but maybe he was right. Maybe it was unfair of her to turn other people's lives upside down for something that was, at this point, only speculation.

Still, she couldn't help but feel disappointed. She'd finally found the courage to confide in Corey about her reasons for coming to Thunder Canyon, foolishly hoping that he would support her quest for the truth. Instead, he was asking her to abandon it.

"Okay," she finally said. "I won't say anything to Grant—"

Corey pressed a brief kiss to her lips before she could finish. "Thank you. The Cliftons have had enough crises to deal without having their lives turned upside by something like this."

She felt uneasy. He'd obviously assumed she was willing to forget about her potential connection to Grant when all she'd intended to say was that she wouldn't mention anything to her boss *until* she had concrete proof of their relationship. Because there was no way she could abandon the quest she'd already started.

They spent the rest of the weekend together, and while Corey had apparently managed to put their conversation aside, it continued to weigh on Erin's mind.

For a minute, when they'd faced off in her kitchen and he'd told her she had to choose, he'd reminded her of Brandon. He'd been her first serious boyfriend, her first lover, and she'd been so infatuated with him she hadn't realized that he was slowly trying to take control of her life. She wasn't allowed to have thoughts and opinions unless they supported his thoughts and opinions. He made suggestions on what she should wear, how she should cut her hair, and he didn't hesitate to express his displeasure when she exhibited her own style choices. He told her he wanted to marry her, but she realized he didn't want a partner but an accessory.

Since then, she'd been careful to steer clear of men with domineering tendencies—until Corey. He was a cowboy through and through, confident and self-assured, the type of man who could walk into any situation and take charge with little effort. He was also attentive, considerate and charming. He listened to her when she talked and he seemed to respect her ideas and opinions. So why had he reacted so strongly—and so negatively—to the possibility that she might be related to Grant?

More importantly—why hadn't she stood up to him? Why hadn't she told him that he had no right to make demands or issue ultimatums? Why hadn't she told him to go to hell?

Because she wanted to believe that he had a valid reason for responding the way he had. Because she wanted to believe that, when she had proof of her claim, he would support her.

Although it carried the same name, Erin knew that the Thunder Canyon General Hospital on White Water Drive wasn't actually the same hospital where she'd been born. The two-story building was less than a dozen years old, having been built during the economic boom to better serve the town's growing population.

But Erin also knew that the records from the old hospital would have been transferred over along with most of the staff. As she stepped beneath the covered portico toward the entrance, she mentally crossed her fingers that if Delores Beckett wasn't still working there, she might at least find someone who could help her track the woman down.

She checked in at the information desk and got directions to the maternity ward on the second floor. As she made her way through the halls, she was surprised by the bright and modern décor. If not for the antiseptic smell and tiled floors, she might have believed she was in an office building rather than a hospital.

The corridor in the maternity wing had a lovely floral border in shades of pink and green and lilac. She stopped at the nurse's station, where a dark-haired nurse wearing blue scrubs decorated with teddy bears was inputting data into a computer.

She looked up and smiled. "Can I help you?"

Erin wiped her suddenly damp palms down the front of her skirt. Now that she was here, she was a bundle of nerves. And she had a sudden urge to turn around and walk away, to "let it go" as Corey had urged her to do.

But she couldn't because she knew that the questions that swirled through her mind would continue to haunt her until she had the answers. Besides, the woman dressed in teddy bears—Beth Ann, according to her name tag—was watching her, waiting.

"I'm, uh, looking for Delores."

Beth Ann glanced at a chart on the wall, but she was already shaking her head. "We only have three new moms here now and no one named Delores. Maybe she went to Billings to have her baby," she suggested helpfully.

"She's not a patient," Erin explained. "She works here."

"Delores?" Beth Ann frowned. "And she works in maternity?"

"Who are you looking for?"

The question came from behind her, and Erin jolted at the sharpness of the tone. Turning, she found herself face-to-face with a tall, steely-eyed doctor.

"Delores—" Her hand went to the scrap of paper in her jacket pocket, the one on which she'd scrawled the nurse's name. Delores Beckett. She didn't need to pull out the paper to verify the name, and she was reluctant to do so. There was something about this doctor's confrontational posture and suspicious glare that made her wary, though she didn't understand why.

Do you think there was some kind of conspiracy? That

the whole town was somehow involved in covering up a baby switch?

Corey's words echoed in the back of her mind, but instead of challenging, this time they sounded like a warning. And while she didn't believe the whole town was involved, it occurred to her that someone other than the nurse might have been aware of the situation. Possibly even the doctor who had delivered the babies.

Erin swallowed. "I knew her before she was married, and I've blanked on her new last name," she fibbed.

"Well, it doesn't matter because we don't have anyone named Delores who works here." The doctor went behind the counter to retrieve a stack of patient charts, effectively dismissing her.

Erin was surprised they had anyone on staff who would be willing to work with such an obnoxiously rude doctor, and even more surprised that anyone would want to give birth in this hospital if it was under his watch.

"Beth Ann—"

The nurse sent Erin an apologetic glance before she turned her attention to the doctor.

"—I need the Warner file."

She closed the cover on the folder beside her computer and held it toward him. He snatched it from her hand and strode away without a backward glance.

"That was Doctor Gifford," Beth Ann said to Erin.

"Friendly guy," she muttered.

The nurse smiled. "This woman you're looking for—" she hesitated "—is it possible that you mean Doris Becker?"

Erin was sure both Erma and her mother had said "Delores," but "Delores" and "Doris" weren't so very different. Maybe Erma had known her as Delores and had introduced her by that name to Betty, but the nurse shortened her name at work. And maybe Erin was grasping at straws again.

But there was something in the tone of Beth Ann's question—it was almost as if the nurse was suggesting that Erin should talk to Doris, as if there was something she wanted her to know but was afraid to say with the disapproving doctor within earshot.

She shook her head, worried that she was starting to see conspiracies where none existed. However, she had nothing to lose by talking to Doris and she certainly didn't have any other leads to follow.

"I've always called her Delores," she finally said. "I forgot that she sometimes goes by Doris."

Beth Ann checked the schedule that was posted on the wall beside her computer. "She's actually off today, but she's working the afternoon shift the rest of the week. That means she starts at three and usually has her first break around four-thirty."

Erin mentally reviewed her own schedule. She usually worked until five, but if she worked through her lunch the next day, she could probably get away a little early and be at the hospital by four-fifteen. "That's great," she said to the nurse. "Thanks."

She left the hospital disappointed but not entirely dejected. Her visit hadn't been as successful as she would have liked, but something about Beth Ann's demeanor had given her new hope.

Was she on the right track now? Or would Doris end up being another dead end?

Hopefully, within twenty-eight hours, she would have the answers to those questions.

Chapter Ten

Corey was invited to Grant and Stephanie's for dinner Monday night. Grant, apparently having heard through the infallible Thunder Canyon grapevine that his friend was seeing a lot of Erin Castro, extended the invitation to include her as well. Corey knew that Erin would be thrilled to join them, and he hesitated only a second before declining on her behalf.

He couldn't forget what she'd said—her ridiculous belief that Grant was her brother. And he felt it was best not to give her any opportunities to poke into his friend's life more than she already had. Not that he believed she'd slip away from the dinner table to rifle through Grant's home looking for nonexistent proof to support her claim. Especially since she'd decided not to follow up on her suspicions.

He felt a twinge of guilt when he remembered that she *had* agreed to back off and a sharper twinge when he recalled that he'd practically demanded it of her.

He'd reacted strongly, impulsively. But he'd known Grant for a long time; he remembered how his friend's world had fallen apart when John Clifton had been killed. Grant's mother, Helen, had lost any interest in ranching when she lost her husband, and she'd eventually taken her daughter with her to Billings, for a new start away from the horrific memories. Grant had stayed. Eventually he and Stephanie—whose father had been killed along with Grant's—had fallen in love. They'd overcome tragedy and heartache and would soon be expanding their family. They deserved to be happy, to feel secure in the life they were building together.

What Erin had suggested was impossible, he truly believed that. But he also believed that telling Grant there was a chance—however minute—that she might be his sister and that Elise might not be another blow to a man who had already dealt with so much. He didn't even want to imagine the effect that such a claim would have on Elise.

Or maybe he was projecting. Maybe the scars from his own life weren't as long buried as he wanted to believe. He knew what it was like to have his whole world change in a heartbeat. It had happened for him and his brothers and sister when their father was killed by an oil rig explosion. He might have only been eight years old at the time, but he remembered, all too clearly, the sense of complete helplessness. And he remembered thinking that he would have done absolutely anything to put things back the way they were—to leave his life unchanged.

He'd experienced that same powerlessness when his four-and-a-half year old nephew, Dillon's son from his first marriage, died. He would have done anything, would have given anything, to save Toby, but of course, nothing could.

Since then, he'd worked hard to control every aspect of his life. He liked to call the shots. He liked to know not just what was happening but to feel as if he had some command over the outcome of a situation. And when Erin had suggested that she might be Grant's sister, all he could think was that she was going to send his friend's world spiraling out of control, and he wasn't willing to sit back and let that happen.

But he wondered now if he'd been unfair to Erin. He knew that she hadn't come to Thunder Canyon to stir up trouble, that her intentions weren't cruel. More, he could tell that she believed what she'd told him. As outrageous as her claims seemed to him, she honestly thought it was possible that someone at the hospital had mixed up babies. And he'd dismissed her suggestion practically out of hand.

He pushed those recriminations aside. He'd done what he thought was best. And in any event, why would Erin want to be preoccupied with the past when they had so much to look forward to in the future—together?

Erin was more than a little distracted at work the next morning. She lost track of what she was supposed to be doing, and when Corey showed up just before noon, she couldn't think of why he might be there.

"Did we have plans for lunch?" She was sure they didn't—she wouldn't have forgotten something like that. But she'd forgotten a lot of things today that she didn't think she would.

"Not yet," Corey said, giving her one of those smiles that never failed to jumpstart her heart. "But I was hoping we could make some."

"I'm sorry," she said, and she was. Even if he didn't have time to go for lunch or coffee, it always perked up her day when he stopped by. And she felt guilty that she was not only brushing him off, but that she couldn't tell him the reason.

"I switched breaks with Carrie and I'm working through lunch so that I can leave early to meet…a friend."

She cringed inwardly at the lie. It was one thing to stretch the truth when she was trying to get information from Beth Ann, and something else entirely when she was talking to the man she was very personally involved with.

But she couldn't tell him the truth because she knew he would try to talk her out of meeting with Doris. And she'd come too far to back out now. She needed to find out what—if anything—Doris could tell her.

She touched his hand. "I won't be late, though. So if you wanted to come by later for dinner…"

He smiled and leaned forward to brush his lips against hers. "I definitely want to come by later for…dinner."

She felt her cheeks flush in response to the deliberate innuendo. It amazed her, after all the time they'd been together and all the things they'd done together, that he could still make her blush.

"What time?" he asked.

"Seven?"

He kissed her again. "I'll be there."

"I know we're encouraged to provide personal service," Trina said, walking past, "but I'd say that goes above and beyond."

Erin managed a smile, but she didn't miss the edge in her coworker's voice. Obviously Trina was still annoyed because Corey had rejected her advances at Erika and Dillon's wedding.

After he'd gone, she forced herself to focus on her work so that Trina wouldn't have anything else to complain about. The afternoon seemed to stretch out interminably, but at last it was three thirty and she started counting down the last half hour of her shift.

Unfortunately, she got caught up on a long-distance call

that seemed as if it would never end. An executive assistant for a wealthy German businessman was trying to make arrangements for a corporate retreat for twenty-two employees. Erin wanted to transfer the call to group bookings, but there was something of a language barrier in their communications and, in the end, she decided it was probably just easier to make the arrangements herself.

By the time she finalized the details and managed to get away from the desk, it was after four o'clock. Thankfully, she didn't run into any more snags between the resort and the hospital.

As a result of his conversation with Grant the night before, Corey had come up with a business proposition that he wanted to discuss with his brother. But when he caught up with Dillon, who was still helping out at the resort, he found that the doctor had a waiting room full of patients—compliments of a nasty seasonal flu that was making the rounds—and a stack of files and insurance forms on his desk—courtesy of his admitted abhorrence for paperwork.

But the nurse snuck him into Dillon's office, promising that the doctor would check in with him as soon as he had a minute. Half an hour later, his brother finally breezed through the door with a cardboard box under one arm and another handful of patient folders under the other.

"Busy place today," Corey said to his brother.

"Please tell me you don't have a fever, nausea or diarrhea."

"I don't have a fever, nausea or diarrhea," Corey repeated obediently. "What I do have is a proposition."

Dillon dropped the box and the files on his desk and glanced at his watch. "Can you outline it in thirty seconds or less?"

"I think we should invest in the resort."

"And twenty-seven seconds to spare," his brother noted.

"I don't expect you to answer right now. I just thought I'd put the idea out there, give you something to think about."

"I will," Dillon promised.

"Then I'll let you get back to your patients."

"Hey—where are you going now?" Dillon asked.

Corey paused at the door. "Why?"

"Any chance you're headed by the hospital? Because I have some samples from the pharmaceutical rep who was in today that I promised to drop off for Dr. Tabry."

"That *you* promised to drop off," Corey echoed.

Dillon picked up the box again, held it out to his brother. "But if you're headed in that direction…"

He was, but only because it had occurred to him that he and Erin had missed a few of the usual steps in the development of their relationship, and he'd decided to remedy that with old-fashioned courting. Because she was making him dinner tonight, he thought it would be appropriate to take her some flowers. Coincidentally, the flower shop was across the street from the General Hospital.

"Do I look like an errand boy?" Corey asked, not willing to accede too easily to his brother's request.

Dillon gave him a once-over. "Now that you mention it."

Corey snatched the box out of his hand. "Fine. But you owe me."

"Add it to my tab."

"I will."

"How about dinner on Saturday?"

"Are you asking me for a date?"

"Smart ass," Dillon muttered.

Corey just grinned.

"I'm inviting you—and Erin—to come over for dinner Saturday night."

"I thought you didn't like Erin."

"I didn't say I didn't like her," Dillon told him. "I said I didn't know her. Maybe if we all spend some time together, that will change."

"I'll check with her and let you know."

This time, it was a younger, blonde woman who was at the nurse's station.

"I was in yesterday trying to track down an old friend," Erin explained, "and the nurse on duty suggested that I come back this afternoon."

"Oh, yes, Beth Ann told me that someone had stopped by looking for Doris Becker."

She nodded.

"That would be me," the nurse told her.

In that moment, Erin realized two things—Doris Becker knew her cover story was a lie, and there was no way she'd been in attendance when Erin was born. In fact, it was likely Erin had been born before Doris.

"I'm sorry—obviously I made a mistake."

"Not necessarily," Doris said and smiled when Erin frowned. "It's quiet in here today. Why don't we go grab a cup of coffee?"

"I don't want to take up any more of your time."

"I've got time," Doris insisted.

So Erin found herself following the nurse down to the cafeteria. Like the rest of the hospital, it was modern and efficient, if somewhat stark. The floor was white, the tables and chairs were blue, but there were lots of tall windows looking into the lobby on one side and outdoors on the other.

Doris led the way to a self-serve beverage station where she poured herself a large cup of dark roast. Erin opted for the same, generously doctoring her cup with milk and sugar. She insisted on paying for their beverages, in appreciation for Doris's time, and they took their cups to a table overlooking the courtyard.

"It's a much better view in the summer," Doris told her. "When everything is lush and green instead of dull and brown."

"It's a nice hospital," Erin said.

"I've only worked here a few months, but I like it. I'm guessing this…friend you were looking for worked here some time ago."

"She was actually a friend of my aunt's. I never even met her—" she paused there but decided that the nurse having been present at her birth didn't require her to alter that statement "—but I thought, since I was in town, I would look her up."

"She was a labor and delivery nurse?"

"Apparently she delivered me."

Doris sipped her coffee. "I think you might be looking for Delores Beckett."

Erin bobbled her cup, sloshing hot coffee over the rim. She grabbed a napkin from the dispenser on the table to mop up the spill.

"I thought I was looking for Delores Beckett, too," she agreed. "But when I mentioned the name Delores, no one seemed to know who I was talking about."

"That's odd." Doris frowned. "Or maybe not so odd."

"What do you mean?"

"There were whispers of a scandal a while back. No one seemed to know exactly what it was about, but the implication was that it could be huge. Then, just as suddenly as the rumors started, they stopped. And Delores Beckett was gone."

"Gone?" Erin asked, startled.

"Early retirement," Doris clarified. "As I understand, everyone thought she would work another ten or more years before she retired, but I guess she had some health issues that prompted her to give up the job early.

"I wasn't even working here then," the nurse continued. "So everything I'm telling you is complete hearsay, but I do remember hearing some rumblings that the administration was worried Delores had said or done something that might result in a lawsuit against the hospital."

Something like mixing up a couple of babies? Erin wondered but only asked, "Do you have any idea how I might get in touch with Delores?"

Doris shook her head. "I don't. I'm sorry. I'm sure personnel would have current contact information, but I don't know that they'd give it out."

"That's okay," Erin said. "I appreciate everything you've told me."

"I gave you a bad impression of a family friend, and I didn't mean to. For what it's worth, everyone who knew Delores only had good things to say about her."

Erin finished her coffee. "Even Dr. Gifford?"

"Dr. Gifford doesn't have good things to say about anyone," Doris told her. Then she asked curiously, "How do you know Dr. Gifford?"

"I don't, but I crossed paths with him when I was here yesterday."

"Well, apparently he worked with Delores a lot. In fact, there was speculation that if the scandal came to light, it might tarnish his stellar reputation, and that's why he turned on her." She shrugged. "Like I said, I've only been here a few months, so I have no idea what he was like before, but I'll admit that I wouldn't be at all disappointed if he followed in Delores's footsteps and took early retirement, too."

Corey considered the usual flower choices as he made his way toward the reception desk in the main lobby of the Thunder Canyon General Hospital.

Carnations? Too casual.

Roses? Too formal.

A mixed bouquet? He shook his head. Too lazy. That was the type of thing that a forgetful husband picked up for his wife at the grocery store when he stopped to grab a quart of milk on his way home and suddenly remembered that it was her birthday/their anniversary/some other occasion.

Orchids? A more thoughtful choice, he decided, but also a little pretentious.

Corey continued to mull over the possibilities after he'd left the pharmaceutical samples for Dr. Tabry.

Tulips? Probably difficult to get in November.

Lilies? A definite possibility, he thought, then did a double take when he saw someone who looked just like Erin walk out of the cafeteria.

No—it wasn't someone who looked just like her, it was Erin.

But what was she doing at the hospital?

Whatever she was doing there, she obviously didn't expect him to be there because she walked right past without even seeing him.

"Erin."

She spun around. "What are you doing here?"

He gestured back toward the reception area. "I promised to drop off a package for Dillon. What are you doing here?"

"Oh. Um."

She wasn't usually at a loss for words and the fact that she was now concerned him.

"You said you were meeting a friend," he reminded her and realized now that she hadn't been telling him the truth. But why would she have lied? And then he had another, even more disturbing thought. "Did you have an appointment? Are you sick?"

"No," she said quickly. "I'm fine."

His heartbeat slowed to something closer to normal. "Then why are you here?"

"I came to see someone in maternity."

Now that the initial wave of panic had subsided, his brain started to clear. She wasn't at the hospital because she was sick, she was visiting someone.

"Your friend had a baby?"

Erin shook her head. She was muddling everything up. No matter how many half-truths she told, they were never going to add up to the whole until she stopped keeping secrets from everyone. Starting with Corey.

"No. I came to see…" She trailed off as she spotted Doris exiting the cafeteria a minute behind her.

"I'm so sorry about that," the nurse said, apologizing for the cell phone call she'd received just as Erin had been saying goodbye.

"No worries," Erin said. "I knew it was time for you to be getting back to work anyway."

"Unfortunately, yes," the nurse agreed, but her eyes shifted from Erin to Corey, her brows winging upward to meet the fringe of her bangs.

Erin had to smile. The first time she'd seen the sexy cowboy, her own reaction had been very similar.

"This is Corey Traub," she told the nurse. Then, to Corey, "And Doris Becker."

Doris shook his proffered hand, smiling. "Any relation to DJ Traub of DJ's Rib Shack?"

"He's my cousin."

"I absolutely love his sauce," Doris said.

"I'm not sure that's one he's heard before," Corey teased, "but I'll be sure to pass it along."

She laughed. "You do that."

"So, are you and Erin old friends?" he asked the nurse.

Doris winked at her. "Oh yeah, we go way back."

Erin knew the nurse was joking, but Corey took her words at face value. Of course he would because Doris's response confirmed the fib Erin had told him earlier.

And somehow the hole she'd started digging so many months before kept getting deeper and deeper, and Erin was beginning to worry that she would end up over her head.

Chapter Eleven

She had to tell him the truth. Tonight.

Erin spooned the sauce over the grilled chicken, then slid the pan into the oven and checked on the rice.

She would never have made it as a spy—she wasn't cut out for a life of deception. Every single untruth she'd told since she'd arrived in Thunder Canyon weighed heavily on her, but none more so than those that she'd told to Corey.

They were lovers, but she knew that true intimacy between two people was about more than a joining of their bodies. It required openness and honesty and a willingness to share their thoughts and dreams. And if she wanted that with Corey, she had to tell him the truth, not only about her meeting with Doris Becker, but also her plans to find Delores Beckett and uncover the truth about what happened at Thunder Canyon General Hospital on the day that she was born.

At six fifty-eight the doorbell rang, making her smile.

Corey was nothing if not punctual.

But as she wiped her hands on a dish towel and made her way down the hall, her heart started to race and the nerves in her belly twisted into knots.

When she opened the door, she saw that he had a bottle of wine in one hand and flowers in the other. Before she could offer to take either, he had his arms wrapped around her and was kissing her breathless.

"Mmm, you smell delicious."

She laughed. "I think what you smell is the chicken."

"The chicken smells good, too," he said, nuzzling her neck, "but you smell even better."

She stepped away from him. "Does that wine need to go in the fridge?"

"Sure." He handed her the bottle, then the flowers. "And those need to go in a vase."

"I think there's one in the kitchen."

She peeked in the oven at the chicken, stirred the rice, then dug a tall, narrow vase out of the back of the cupboard.

It had been a long time since anyone had brought her flowers, and she was touched by the gesture. She untied the bow, then unwrapped the paper and sighed when she saw the snowy white calla lilies inside.

"Oh, they're gorgeous."

"The florist said they were 'timelessly beautiful.' I thought that described you as much as the flowers."

She traced a finger around the outside of one snowy white trumpet, her eyes misting with tears.

"What's wrong?"

She shook her head. "I guess I'm just feeling a little sentimental," she explained. "My aunt Erma was a big fan of lilies."

"Then she'd probably suggest you put them in water."

She smiled. "I'll do that."

She turned on the faucet and filled the vase, then cut the long, thick stems and carefully arranged the flowers in the water. "So what did I do to deserve these?"

He wrapped his arms around her from behind. "Maybe it's not what you did but what I'm hoping you'll do."

"You think you're going to get lucky tonight?"

"I'm hoping."

She turned to brush her lips against his. "Your chances were pretty good, even without the flowers."

His hands skimmed up her back, down again. "Any chance of getting lucky before dinner?"

She was tempted to say "yes," to take him by the hand and lead him up to her bedroom. When they were together, when their bodies were linked and their hearts were pounding in unison, it was as if the rest of the world didn't exist. Nothing else mattered, certainly not some regrettable half-truths and misunderstood evasions.

But after her conversation with Doris, she'd been more determined than ever to find Delores Beckett and learn the truth about what happened at the hospital on the day she was born. And because that truth might very well affect other people in Thunder Canyon—people who were friends of Corey's—she had to tell him about her intentions. Even if she knew that he would disapprove.

"Not if you want dinner to be edible," she warned, and ducked out of his embrace.

"I'm really not that hungry," he assured her.

But she was already taking the pan of chicken out of the oven and Corey inhaled deeply, then sighed. "Mmm, that does smell good."

He reached into the cupboard to get the plates for her.

"I thought you weren't that hungry," she teased.

"Well, since you've gone to so much trouble, we should eat."

She dished up the chicken and rice while he opened the wine. Conversation during dinner was easy, casual. Erin wanted to tell him what she'd learned from Doris, but there didn't seem to be any natural segue into that topic of conversation. Or maybe she was more chicken than what was on her plate.

Corey was up to his elbows in soapy water when the bell rang. Though Erin had insisted that the dishes could wait, he figured a little washing up was the least he could do to repay her for another fabulous meal. Plus he wanted to make sure that once he got her upstairs, she wouldn't be distracted by thoughts of dirty plates and glasses in the sink downstairs.

Not that he had any doubts about being able to keep her mind as thoroughly occupied as her body—or any shortage of ideas on how to do so.

"I'll get it," Erin said.

He watched her walk down the hall toward the door, enjoying the subtle sway of her hips beneath the slim skirt she was wearing. She really had a great butt. And fabulous legs. And when she was dressed in one of those neat little suits she usually wore to work, he couldn't help but think about how much fun he would have getting her out of it. Because beneath all that buttoned-up style was a warm and passionate woman.

Of course, she dressed more casually on her days off and was equally appealing in faded denim and fuzzy sweaters. Even more appealing in nothing at all. He pushed those thought aside and dried his hands just as Erin opened the door.

"Are you Erin Castro?" the visitor, a sixtyish woman, asked.

He had come around through the living room, and he could see the wariness in Erin's expression.

"Yes, I am. Who are you?"

"I'm Delores. Delores Beckett."

The name meant nothing to him, but obviously it meant something to Erin because her eyes went wide and her breath caught.

"Oh. I didn't—I mean—how—why—*what* are you doing here?"

"I heard you were looking for me," Delores said.

"I was. I am." Erin was obviously flustered, and her gaze went from the older woman to him and back again, her eyes narrowing. "It *was* you. I spoke to you on the phone."

"Yes," Delores admitted. "But I wasn't sure who you were or what you wanted then. It wasn't until after I'd hung up that I made the connection between the aunt you mentioned and Erma and finally realized why you were looking for me."

Of course, Corey still didn't know why Erin had been looking for Delores, but he had an uneasy feeling—bolstered by her refusal to meet his gaze—that he wasn't going to like the answer to that question.

"Will you come in, please?" Erin invited.

The older woman stepped into the foyer.

"Do you want me to make coffee?" Corey asked.

Erin seemed surprised by the offer—or maybe she'd forgotten he was there, which meant that his plans for the rest of the evening had taken a sudden detour.

"This is Corey Traub—a friend of mine," Erin told Delores. Then, to him, "Delores was a friend of my aunt Erma's."

"Coffee would be great," Delores said to him.

"I'll put it on," he told her.

"Thanks," Erin said.

When the coffee had finished brewing and they sat down together in the kitchen, it occurred to Corey that whatever Erin wanted to discuss with her visitor had nothing to do with him. But he was afraid that if he offered to leave, she would let him and he would never find out what was going on. Because he knew that there was something going on, something she hadn't told him.

Like Heather.

No, he wasn't going to go there. He wasn't going to assume that Erin had deliberately kept anything from him. She wouldn't do that.

"How did you find me?" Erin asked Delores now.

"Reverse lookup."

"Obviously you're not as opposed to technology as my aunt was," Erin said, smiling just a little.

Delores chuckled. "I'm an old woman who lives alone with a cat and a computer—I'm a registered member of twenty-nine chatrooms."

"You live alone? But I saw a young woman and a little girl…" Her words trailed off, her cheeks turned pink.

"My daughter and granddaughter." Delores smiled. "And I thought that was probably you parked across the street last Wednesday."

Corey didn't say anything, but he also didn't fail to make the connection between the date and the memory of Erin brushing off his invitation to go riding that same afternoon. Of course, he hadn't realized she was brushing him off or that her purpose had been to stake out this grandmother.

"Well, thank you for finding me," Erin said. "Because I was beginning to give up hope that I would ever locate you."

"I'm sure you have questions," Delores said. "And I've got some explaining to do."

Explaining? *That* definitely caught his attention.

Erin's gaze shifted to his again. "Delores isn't just a friend of my aunt's," she told him. "She was also the nurse who was working in labor and delivery at Thunder Canyon General Hospital the night I was born."

Erin could practically see all of the pieces click together in Corey's mind, but she wasn't going to worry about his reaction right now. She would explain everything to him later—after she got the answers to her questions from Delores.

"How did you know Erma?" she asked.

It wasn't the foremost question on her mind, but she wasn't quite ready to dive headfirst into the murky waters of her birth. She was still feeling a little unsettled by the knowledge that the woman who could answer her questions was sitting in her kitchen. The truth was finally within her grasp, and she wasn't entirely sure that she was ready for it.

"I grew up in the house next door to where she and Irwin lived," Delores explained. "I was just a kid, but she always took the time to talk to me. She knew more about my life and my friends and my ambitions than my own mother, and I was devastated when she left Thunder Canyon. I only saw her a few times after she moved away, but we kept in touch faithfully if not regularly.

"Then I had a stroke last February," she continued. "It was mild, as far as those things go, but it made me realize that I wasn't going to live forever. If I wanted to confess my sins, so to speak, I needed to do so before it was too late. So I went to visit Erma.

"She told me that she was going to tell you what happened

at the hospital the night you were born. But then, when she passed away and I didn't hear from you, I wasn't sure she had."

"What did happen?" Erin asked. "Did you mix up the babies?"

Delores's eyes filled with tears. "I don't know, but I'm not sure that I didn't."

She glanced at Corey. His cool, narrow-eyed stare proved he was angry that she'd continued to pursue investigating exactly this possibility when he'd asked her not to, but she had to trust that he would understand once he realized she was only trying to find the truth.

"Can you tell me exactly what happened?" she asked Delores.

"There were two women in labor that day, and they gave birth literally within minutes of each other. Not an unusual occurrence in a bigger hospital, but hardly commonplace in Thunder Canyon. Plus, we were short-staffed that night, so I was assisting both deliveries.

"Everything seemed fine, but then one of the mothers starting hemorrhaging, and suddenly there was chaos. Dr. Gifford took her into surgery and I took the baby to the nursery."

Dr. Gifford? Erin only had a moment to register that the rumors were true—that the scandal everyone at the hospital had been whispering about could tarnish the doctor's good reputation—before Delores forged ahead with her story.

"Now we have computer-printed labels and the ID bracelets are snapped around the babies' ankles before they're ever taken out of the delivery room," she explained. "But back then, the attending nurse printed the information by hand. That's what I was doing when I was called out to assess another mother who had been admitted in the early stages of labor.

"I was only gone a few minutes, but when I came back, both of the babies were gone. A young nurse, new on staff and trying to be helpful, had taken them down to the nursery, not realizing that I had yet to put the ID bracelets on either one."

Erin was frustrated that such a mistake had been made, but there was no doubt in her mind that it was a mistake. Neither Delores nor the other young nurse had any malicious intent, and she didn't think it was fair that Delores had essentially been forced into retirement because of the mistake.

And as much as she hadn't been impressed with Dr. Gifford during their brief meeting, she didn't want his career to be ruined over something that had happened twenty-six years before. She just wanted to make things right—except that wasn't possible now.

There was no way to go back in time and ensure that Betty Castro and Helen Clifton had gone home with the right babies—if, in fact, they had not done so. Right now, Erin was so confused, she wasn't sure what she believed.

You need to find your family. They're in Thunder Canyon.

She didn't doubt that Erma believed it was true.

And in her heart, she believed it, too. The first day that she'd driven into Thunder Canyon, she'd felt as if she was finally home; the first time she'd been introduced to Grant Clifton, she'd felt a connection, as if she knew him even though they'd never met before.

She'd also felt worry and guilt, wondering what her search for the truth would mean for the family she'd grown up with, for the parents and brothers who had always loved her even if they didn't always understand her.

She loved them, too, and the very last thing she ever wanted to do was hurt them. But she also knew that she couldn't ignore the truth. She couldn't pretend the mistake hadn't been made. She didn't want to. She wanted to know Grant as her brother; she wanted to meet his mother—the woman who had given birth to her.

And what about what they wanted?

Although he hadn't said anything in a while, it was Corey's voice that she heard, asking the question that echoed in the back of her mind.

What if they only wanted to enjoy the status quo and not have their entire lives turned upside down?

And she couldn't help but wonder, "How could someone leave the hospital with the wrong baby?"

"Neither mother thought she had the wrong baby—no one had any reason to suspect that a mix-up may have occurred."

"I guess I just thought that, after carrying a baby for nine months, there would be a natural bond between mother and child."

"The maternal bond is an amazing thing," Delores said. "But it's not always instantaneous. It can happen within minutes or it can take days or weeks, especially if the mother and child are separated for some reason immediately following the birth."

"As happened when my mother was taken into surgery," Erin guessed.

Delores nodded. "She was in rough shape for a few days after that, and by then, Helen Clifton had already left the hospital with her daughter."

"Still, you could have said something then," Erin said. "You could have admitted there might have been a mix-up and fixed it then."

"I could have," Delores agreed sadly. "And I should have. But I was scared, terrified. It had been my mistake—I would have lost my job. And it didn't seem like any real harm had been done. After all, both mothers went home with beautiful baby girls."

"That's how you justified it?"

Delores looked down at the hands she'd wrapped around her mug. "I'm not proud of what I did. And not a day has gone by in the past twenty-six years that I haven't thought I should have done things differently. But the longer I waited, the harder it was to admit my mistake. If it even was a mistake."

"Did you tell anyone what had happened?"

"Dr. Gifford. We didn't only work together, we were... involved. He urged me to keep quiet, insisting that no one would ever find out what I'd done. I was sure he was wrong, that someone would start asking questions.

"I didn't sleep for days. But then, as the weeks turned into months, I started to think maybe he was right. As the months turned into years, it seemed more and more believable that no one would ever know.

"But I knew. And the longer I held on to the secret, the more it ate away at me, haunted me.

"I knew where both of the babies were. Elise Clifton had grown up in Thunder Canyon, so I knew that—despite her father's tragic death—she had a family who loved her. And through my correspondence with Erma, I knew that the same was true about you. But then Erma began to make comments that caused me to worry that everything wasn't as great as I wanted to think."

"What kind of comments?" Erin asked, curious.

"She said that your parents didn't understand you, that if she hadn't been there when you were born, she'd have thought you were left on their doorstep."

"Do you think she knew?"

"I don't know how she could have." She paused, as if considering the possibility, then smiled. "And yet, Erma seemed to have a knack for seeing things others didn't—that's why people called her crazy.

"And then, when I went to see her in the spring, when I told her that I might have mixed up the babies, she said, 'Well, that explains everything.' To her, it wasn't a possibility but a fact."

"I know she was adamant that my family was in Thunder Canyon," Erin said.

Delores nodded. "She told me that she was going to tell you what happened all those years ago. I've been waiting on pins and needles for months, expecting that any day you would show up."

"I didn't get the whole story from Erma, only a few pieces that I struggled—unsuccessfully—to put together. That's why I came to Thunder Canyon, to try to get more information. I didn't even remember your name until my mother mentioned it. And when I couldn't track you down through the telephone listings, I decided to go to the hospital, looking for someone who might be able to help me find you. As it turns out, I ran into Dr. Gifford when I was there."

"And he pretended he'd never even heard my name," the nurse guessed.

"He certainly didn't give any indication that he'd worked with you."

"David excels at nothing more so than covering his own behind," Delores said. "Not that I can blame him, in this case. He only knew about the possibility of a mix-up because I told him. He wasn't there—he'd gone into surgery with Betty. And he wasn't responsible for ID'ing the babies—that was my job."

"But he encouraged you to keep quiet about your concerns." Erin didn't quite manage to keep the bitterness out of her tone.

Delores didn't make any more excuses for her former lover. "And now that you know, what do you plan to do about it?"

"I guess we need to prove that the mistake was made."

"You're sure that's what you want to do?"

"Of course."

"And are you prepared for the consequences whatever the truth may be? Because if it's true that I put the wrong bracelet on the wrong baby, that Helen Clifton gave birth to you and Betty Castro gave birth to Elise, then the truth is going to turn a lot of lives upside down."

Erin was quiet for a long time after Delores had gone.

Corey left her alone, figuring she needed some time to fully assimilate everything she had learned. He finished tidying up the kitchen while he tried to do the same.

He may not have grown up in Thunder Canyon, but he had family and friends in this town. They were a close-knit community, and this kind of news—if it was true—could devastate them. It would certainly devastate Grant and Elise.

"You haven't said anything," Erin noted softly.

"I don't know what to say," he admitted. "All I can think is that you lied to me."

She winced but didn't deny it.

"You told me you were going to forget your theory about babies being switched," he said.

"No, I didn't—at least, not intentionally. I only meant to promise that I wouldn't say anything to Grant until I had proof."

"You didn't say anything about continuing to look for proof."

"Because you didn't give me a chance."

"So it's *my* fault you lied to me?"

She sighed. "No. I should have made my intentions clear. But you were being so unreasonable and—" She cut herself off, as if realizing that being critical of his attitude wasn't an effective defense of her own actions. "It doesn't matter. I should have been honest."

"Yes, you should have," he said. "And now you're still determined to drag all of this out into the open, aren't you?"

"'All of this' happens to be my life. I need to know who I am," she insisted.

"Delores admitted that she *may* have put the wrong ID bracelet on the wrong baby. Even she can't say for sure that she did. I'm willing to admit that it's possible that she got the babies mixed up. Why can't you admit the possibility that she didn't?"

"Because there are too many coincidences to ignore, and because Elise looks more like my brothers than I do."

"But what purpose can be served by bringing a twenty-six-year-old mistake to light now?"

"How about the truth?"

"But at what cost?"

She frowned at that.

"Erin, if you go to anyone with your suspicions—whether it's your parents or Grant—there are a lot of people who will be hurt."

"Do you really think it would be better if I didn't say anything? Do you really believe the truth can be buried forever?"

"I'm wondering if a woman who could deceive so many people so easily can even recognize the truth," he told her.

She recoiled as if she'd been slapped. He hadn't intended to hurt her, but he couldn't just stand back and watch as she hurt other people—people he cared about.

"Because the truth may be that Delores Beckett was distracted from her duties the day you were born but still managed to put the right ID bracelet on the right baby," he continued.

"No one else has any clue what's going on—not your parents or Grant or Elise or their mother. You've had *months* to think about this, to put all the pieces together. Do you really think they're going to be happy when you start throwing around these allegations?"

"You can't understand how I feel," she told him. "Because you know exactly where you fit into your family, but I can't make plans for my future when I have so many unanswered questions about my past."

"I can't—I *won't*—be a part of this. If you insist on following through with this, you're on your own."

Her eyes—those beautiful blue eyes that could never hide her feelings—were filled with anguish. "Don't do this, Corey. Please."

"I'm not doing anything."

"You're forcing me to make an impossible choice," she told him.

"Is it impossible? Or has your choice already been made?"

She looked away but not before he saw the shimmer of her tears. "I guess it has."

He left without saying anything else.

From his perspective, there was nothing left to say.

Chapter Twelve

Erin didn't know what to think when she was called into Grant's office the next day.

At first, she'd worried that Corey might have gone to her boss after he'd left her condo the night before, but she dismissed that idea almost as quickly as it had come to her. Corey had been adamant that he wouldn't have any part in bringing to light the information she'd obtained from Delores Beckett.

"Is everything okay?" her boss asked.

"That's what I was going to ask you," Erin said.

Grant smiled, but he still looked concerned. "You seem a little...preoccupied today."

"I'm sorry—"

"I don't want an apology. I want to know if there's anything I can do to help."

She could only shake her head, not meeting his gaze.

"You're a good employee, Erin. An asset to the resort.

And if you're dissatisfied with any part of your job, I want to know."

She looked up now. "I love working here," she assured him.

"Then it's personal," he guessed.

She nodded.

"And none of my business?"

She wanted to open up to him, but she didn't know what to say. It was hardly the time or the place to tell him that she believed his mother had also given birth to her.

Now that she'd spoken with Delores Beckett, she was closer than ever to the answers she'd come to Thunder Canyon to find. But in her search for the truth, she'd found something she'd never expected to find—and lost it. And when Corey had walked out on her the night before, he'd taken her heart with him.

"Just not anything you can help me with," she told him.

"Okay," he said. "But I want you to know that I have an open-door policy here, and I hope that you'll come to me if there's ever anything you think I can help you with."

"Thank you. I will."

"On another topic," he said. "It's my sister's twenty-sixth birthday on the twentieth."

She nodded. "You mentioned that at Erika and Dillon's wedding."

He seemed surprised that she would have remembered. She probably wouldn't have if not for the fact that it was her birthday on the same day, but of course he didn't know that.

"Anyway, I thought if you weren't doing anything, you might want to come. I've already invited Corey—"

"Corey and I—we aren't dating any more," she told him.

"Oh," Grant said, in a sympathetic tone that suggested he suddenly understood why she'd been distracted. "Well, there will be other people there, too, and Stephanie and I would like you to come."

"That's very kind of both of you," Erin said. "But I don't even know your sister."

"Elise and my mom have been living in Billings for so long now that there are a lot of people in town that she doesn't know, but I'm hoping this party will give her the opportunity to get to know them and maybe entice her to move back to Thunder Canyon," he admitted.

"You must miss her a lot."

"I do. It's hard to play the annoying big brother when she's so far away."

Erin managed a smile. "I have two big brothers—they seem to manage even from a distance."

Grant chuckled. "Elise would probably say the same thing about me."

"I'd like to meet her."

"Then you'll come to the party? We're taking over DJ's at seven o'clock for the event, so you know the food will be good."

"I'll think about it." Erin stood up. "But right now I should get back to work before my boss catches me slacking off."

"I'll put in a good word for you." Grant walked with her to the door, pausing with his hand on the knob. "Corey and I have been friends for a long time, but if he doesn't come to his senses soon, there are plenty of other single guys in this town that I could introduce you to. And a lot of them will be at the party."

"I appreciate the offer but—"

"None of my business," he filled in for her.

She smiled to show that she wasn't offended, then ducked out of his office before she burst into tears and completely humiliated herself.

Corey decided to head to The Hitching Post on Monday night to grab a beer and maybe find someone to shoot some pool with. He needed a distraction—something to help him forget about Erin and all of her lies. His mind kept replaying the scene between Delores and Erin, but he was still having trouble accepting that the nurse's story had confirmed Erin's suspicions. Maybe he'd been hasty in dismissing the suggestion that she could be Grant's sister, and maybe it had been unfair to expect her to leave the past in the past. But in the end, what he couldn't forget—what he couldn't forgive—were her lies.

Every day that passed and she didn't tell him the truth, she'd lied. He felt angry and betrayed. And maybe he was hurting, too, because when it came right down to it and she'd had to make a choice, she hadn't chosen him.

He pushed open the door and was greeted by a familiar country song about a woman who'd done a cowboy wrong. Yeah, he'd come to the right place. Or so he thought until a cursory glance around the room showed his brother having dinner with his new family.

He moved toward the bar.

The last thing he needed tonight was an invitation to join Dillon and his bride and their two-year-old daughter. Technically Emilia was Dillon's stepdaughter, of course, but Corey knew his brother didn't think of the little girl that way. When he'd married Erika, she'd become his wife and her daughter had become his daughter, too. Dillon didn't seem to care about Erika's past relationship or the man who had fathered her child.

It was probably one of the reasons Corey found it difficult to understand why Erin was so obsessed with knowing who gave birth to her when, by her own admission, she had a family who loved her. Why wasn't it enough that he loved her, too?

Of course, he hadn't actually spoken those words to her. He'd never had a chance to tell her what was in his heart. Would the words have changed anything between them? He didn't know.

He was on his second beer when Dillon slid onto the vacant stool beside him. Corey looked around but didn't see any sign of his brother's wife or child.

"Erika took Emilia home," Dillon answered the unspoken question. "It's long past her bedtime."

"So why are you still here?"

"Because you don't look like you should be drinking alone." He signaled to Carl, who was tending the bar tonight, for a draft beer.

"I'm fine," Corey said.

The statement was so blatantly untrue that his brother didn't even bother to dispute it. "How are the evaluations at Rycon coming along?"

"Fine."

With a nod of thanks to the bartender, Dillon picked up the mug that had been set in front of him. "How about your discussion with Grant about the Resort?"

"Fine," Corey said again.

"How's Erin?"

"Look, Dillon, as much as I appreciate the brotherly concern, I really wish you'd just go home to your new family and leave me the hell alone."

Dillon nodded. "So she *is* the reason you look like you want to knock some heads together."

"And if you insist on hanging around here, yours might be the first."

"I'm not worried," his brother said. "Because as often as we've gone head-to-head, I've always had your back, and I know you've always had mine."

Corey sighed, silently damning his brother because he spoke the truth. And because it was true, because Dillon had always been there for him, he wouldn't get any satisfaction from turning on him now.

"So are you going to tell me what happened to make you so miserable?"

"Let's just say that I learned something I didn't want to know."

"Everyone has secrets," Dillon said.

"Weren't you the one who warned me about Erin's?"

His brother shrugged. "Only because I know you have a tendency to leap before you look."

He didn't say 'Like with Heather,' but they were both thinking it.

He'd met Heather while he was in college. She was the first woman he'd ever fallen in love with and he'd actually thought they would get married someday. One of the things he liked about her was that she didn't expect him to pay her way just because he was rich. Unlike several other women he'd dated, she prided herself on supporting herself through her job as a waitress. At least, that's what she'd told him she did. He later found out that she wasn't waiting tables but dancing on them, and it wasn't an exclusive upscale restaurant but a private men's club.

He didn't care that she'd taken off her clothes for money. Not that he was thrilled to think of all the men who had stared at and undoubtedly lusted for her naked body, but he didn't blame her for taking a job that paid her bills. He couldn't forgive her for lying, though.

After his experience with Heather, he had no tolerance for half-truths. Maybe Erin hadn't actually lied to him, but her failure to tell him the whole truth was just as much a breach of trust. He'd been played for a fool...again. And he was as furious as he was hurt by her deception.

"But in retrospect, I may have been too quick to pass judgment," Dillon was saying now.

"You weren't," Corey told him.

"And maybe you are, too."

He frowned.

"The thing is, Erika and Erin are really close, and Erika isn't easily taken in."

"As you learned when she kept saying 'no' to you," Corey couldn't resist teasing, although the effort was half-hearted.

His brother shrugged. "As a single mother with a young child, she had reason to be wary. But she never had any misgivings about Erin."

Maybe she should have, he thought, but he didn't say the words aloud because he didn't want to cause his brother undue concern. After all, Erin's reasons for being in Thunder Canyon really wouldn't affect the life Dillon was building here with Erika and Emilia.

"Do you ever think about Emilia's biological father?" he asked.

"Of course," Dillon answered without hesitation.

"Okay—fast forward twenty years and think about how you would react if the daughter you'd raised since she was two years old suddenly told you she wanted to know her father."

Dillon sipped his beer, considering. "I'd hope I could be supportive," he finally said.

"Wouldn't you think she was...ungrateful?"

His brother shook his head. "Six months ago, I might

have given you a different answer." He smiled. "Of course, six months ago, I didn't know Erika or Emilia. But Peter's recent heart attack has made me see a lot of things differently. Now I can appreciate everything he did over the years. Not just as a husband to Mom, but as a father to six kids he had no biological tie to. I can also see how tough it has been for some of the others—Rose, in particular—to have no memory of the man who contributed half of her DNA, and I can understand that the not knowing can leave a void no one else can see."

Corey finished his beer and shook his head when Carl looked over to see if he wanted another refill.

...the not knowing can leave a void...

Maybe that was what Erin had meant when she said that she needed to know her past before she could plan her future.

But her lies had undermined the foundation of what was between them, and Corey couldn't forgive her for that.

Erin couldn't go to a birthday party empty-handed, but never having met the guest of honor made it difficult to know what kind of gift might be appropriate. She wandered through the resort shops on her lunch hour, hoping something would catch her eye. What finally did was a collage-style picture frame with the word "Family" etched in the bottom corner of the glass.

She wondered at the irony that would have her give such a gift to a woman whose family she might tear apart with the information she had. But that wasn't her intention. Yes, things would change—for both Erin and Elise—but she refused to look at it as a negative. She had no intention of walking away from Betty and Jack and her brothers if it turned out that Betty Castro hadn't given birth to her, and she certainly wouldn't expect Elise to turn her back on Helen or Grant.

As the salesclerk wrapped the gift, Erin continued to wander through the store. She paused at a display of decorative perfume bottles and caught a glimpse of someone through the store window. For one brief, heart-stopping moment, she thought it was Corey. But then the man turned to speak to the woman at his side, and she saw that it was actually his brother, Dillon, with his new wife. Erika smiled at something her husband said, then he bent his head and kissed her gently.

Erin felt a pang in her heart, and she had to look away from the obvious love between them. She'd started to think that she'd found something similar with Corey. She'd let herself believe that if Erika could find love, maybe she could, too.

Obviously she'd been wrong.

Corey hadn't expected that Erin would show up at the birthday party Grant was hosting for his sister. He wouldn't have thought she'd have the nerve. But not only did she come, she came with Erika and Dillon.

And when she walked through the door, his heart knocked hard against his ribs, forcing him to admit how much he'd missed her. It had only been a few days since he'd last seen her, since he'd learned of her deception, but those few days had seemed like a lifetime.

He noticed that she'd brought a gift—a good way to get an introduction to the birthday girl, he figured, then remembered that Erin should be celebrating her birthday today, too.

She set the wrapped package on a table that had been set aside for that purpose and unbuttoned her coat. As she shrugged it off of her shoulders and turned to hang it on a hook, he nearly choked on the beer he'd been about to swallow.

She was wearing a dress. He wasn't sure he'd ever seen her in a dress before—other than the day of Dillon and Erika's wedding, of course. She often wore skirts to work, but he'd never seen her in something so flirty and feminine. There were no sleeves, so her long, slender arms were bare, and the short, fluttery skirt showed off miles of shapely leg.

She looked…stunning.

As if sensing his perusal, she turned. They were separated by the width of the room, but even over that distance their eyes met, held. And then she looked away.

Corey lifted his glass to his lips again, then realized it was empty. He went back to the bar, but this time he ordered a Coke. He obviously didn't need alcohol fogging his brain when just being in the same room with Erin had the same effect.

If he'd expected that she would be so devastated by their breakup that she'd be hiding out in her condo, he was obviously mistaken. Of course, why would she be devastated? She was the one who'd decided their relationship was over.

He watched her hips sway as she walked, appreciating the way her soft, flowing skirt swirled around her thighs as she moved. Unfortunately, just admiring those legs from a distance reminded him of how they'd felt wrapped around him—

He turned away, mortified to realize that he was getting aroused just thinking about her.

Of course, the physical parts of their relationship had been phenomenal. Everything between them had clicked.

He'd thought they were clicking in other areas, too.

They'd had so much fun, talking and laughing and just being together.

And then he'd found out about her lies, and he'd realized they had nothing if they didn't have trust.

But the heart didn't always defer to the logic of the mind, and, although he told himself that she was just like Heather, his heart wouldn't accept that it was true.

Because he loved her.

Regardless of what she'd said and done—or not said and failed to do—his heart urged him to give her another chance, to give *them* another chance.

The first time he'd set eyes on her, he'd felt something stir inside of him. He hadn't even known her name, but he'd somehow known that she was the woman he was meant to be with. And so he'd pursued her, relentlessly and single-mindedly.

And then he'd found out that she wasn't quite the woman he'd wanted her to be, that she had secrets he couldn't have guessed and didn't want to believe. And still, he couldn't shake the feelings he had for her. He couldn't stop wanting her, needing her, loving her.

But he'd abandoned her when she needed him. All she'd asked for was some compassion and understanding, and he'd turned on her because he didn't want to rock the boat. It wasn't even *his* boat, but the peacemaking instinct of the middle child was so deeply ingrained in him it had a tendency to carry over to all areas of his life. How ironic that his desire to maintain the status quo for his friend's family had led to his conflict with Erin.

Maybe it wasn't about giving her a second chance but asking if she would give him one.

…I can't make plans for my future when I have so many unanswered questions about my past.

He didn't think she'd actually come here tonight to answer those questions, but maybe he should stick close to her—just to be sure.

Erin didn't feel as awkward as she thought she would at Elise Clifton's party. Although she'd never met Grant's sister, she was surprised by how many of the guests she did know. Obviously she'd met more people and made more friends than she'd realized during the few months that she'd been in Thunder Canyon.

In fact, she didn't feel uncomfortable at all except for that brief moment when she'd glanced around the room and found Corey watching her. She'd known he would be there, but she hadn't expected that she would feel so rattled by his presence.

But she should have. After all, they'd been more than casual acquaintances—they'd been lovers. And although their time together had been brief, it had also been more intimate and intense than any other relationship Erin had ever had.

Of course, that was over now, she reminded herself. And although she might regret the way their relationship had ended, there was no point in wishing things had turned out differently. She couldn't deny herself the answers she'd sought for so long just because he wanted her to. And the fact that he could even ask it of her, knowing how important it was to her to find the truth, proved that he didn't care about her half as much as he'd claimed.

Anyway, it was inevitable that, in a town the size of Thunder Canyon, she would cross paths with Corey every now and again. And she was relieved that the first meeting had happened. They hadn't actually exchanged words, but she was okay with that. She was still too raw to be able to hide the hurt she was feeling.

She wandered around the buffet table, more out of curiosity than hunger, examining the assortment of finger foods. Her stomach was too knotted to contemplate putting anything into it right now, but she might eat later, when Corey was gone—or at least when he stopped watching her.

Was she being paranoid—or was he shadowing her every move? Probably he was sticking close so he could intervene if she got too close to one of his friends.

But he didn't make a move when Grant and Stephanie sought her out, or even when Grant pulled his mother and his sister over to meet her.

Truthfully, Erin wouldn't have minded if he'd interrupted just then because coming face-to-face with Elise Clifton for the first time, she was absolutely speechless. It wasn't just that the resemblance to her own brothers was more evident in person—it was the tiny brown birthmark on the side of Elise's nose, exactly where Jake and Josh each had identical birthmarks.

Erin hadn't noticed the birthmark in the photo, or maybe the angle from which the picture was taken had hidden it from view. But she knew that the presence of that birthmark couldn't possibly be a coincidence—it had to mean that Elise was Betty and Jack Castro's child.

After Grant had made the introductions, while Erin was still reeling from the shock of this revelation, Helen Clifton looked at her thoughtfully.

"Would your mother be Betty Castro by any chance?" she asked.

Erin's heart was pounding hard and fast as she faced the woman who had not raised her but who, she was now certain, had given birth to her. But she could hardly say, 'Actually, you're my mother,' and because Betty had been her mother in every other way, she answered, "Yes, she is."

"Erin's mother and I gave birth on the same day, practically at the same time, right here in Thunder Canyon," Helen informed them.

"No birthing horror stories, please," Stephanie said quickly.

"I don't have any to tell," the older woman assured her expectant daughter-in-law.

"Good." Stephanie breathed a sigh of relief as she rubbed her baby bump. "But just in case, I'll excuse myself to get this rapidly growing baby some food."

"I'll make sure she skips the seafood and sits while she eats," Grant said, following his wife.

"If your mom gave birth the same day as mine, then it's your birthday today, too," Elise said to Erin after her brother and sister-in-law had gone.

She nodded, feeling more than a little self-conscious that the attention had shifted in her direction.

"Are your parents here to celebrate with you?" Helen asked. "It would be a hoot to see your mother again."

"No," Erin said. Despite this most recent and shocking revelation—or maybe because of it—she realized she missed her family more than ever. "They live in San Diego, but they are coming for Thanksgiving."

"Well, maybe we'll have a chance to get together while they're here."

"In the meantime," Elise said, "I should see if someone in the kitchen can add your name to the cake."

"No." The protest was as immediate as it was instinctive.

"Why not?" Elise asked.

"Because this is *your* party."

"But it's *our* birthday."

She was so gracious and generous and her easy acceptance made Erin feel all the more guilty about the secrets she carried deep inside.

"That's really kind," Erin said, "but—"

"But we need to be going," Corey interjected, touching a hand to her back. "We have another birthday celebration to attend."

While she was grateful to have been rescued, she wasn't entirely sure how she felt about Corey being her rescuer. But she was desperate enough to escape that she played along.

"Oh. Of course," Elise said, though she sounded more than a little disappointed.

"Enjoy the rest of your night," Erin said and impulsively hugged her.

Grant's sister hugged her back; then Helen did, too.

"It was a pleasure to meet you—again," she said and laughed.

Erin forced a smile, but her throat was tight and her eyes were stinging.

Corey said his goodbyes, then ushered her toward the exit.

"I'll grab your coat," he said.

She only nodded.

He slipped the garment over her shoulders and guided her out of the restaurant.

"Why did you do that?" she finally asked him.

He shrugged. "You looked like you needed to get out of there."

"I did," she admitted. "Thanks."

"What are you thinking now? Do you still believe Delores made a mistake at the hospital?"

"I know she did," Erin told him.

He frowned. "Why are you suddenly so certain?"

"Because Elise has a little birthmark on her face in exactly the same spot that both of my brothers do."

He didn't say anything.

Erin pulled her wallet out of her purse. Her fingers trembled as she pulled out photos of each of her brothers. "Look."

Corey did, his frown deepening.

"Are you thinking that this is yet another coincidence?" she asked.

"No, I'm wondering why you didn't say anything in there," he admitted.

She stared at him. "Did you really think I would just blurt something like that out? Is that why you're here? To make sure I didn't cause a scene?"

"I'm here because I was invited."

"So why were you hovering around me rather than visiting with your friends?"

"Because the minute I saw you walk through the door, darlin', I realized how much I've missed you."

Her traitorous heart bumped against her ribs. She couldn't do this—she couldn't let him get to her. She didn't have any emotional reserves left to deal with him right now.

"You were the one who walked out," she reminded him.

"I made a mistake."

Oh, she wanted to believe him. She needed to feel as if she had someone on her side when all of her family allegiances suddenly seemed so uncertain. But he'd hurt her already, and her heart was still feeling too bruised to endure another beating.

"Look, I appreciate the rescue in there, but if you don't mind, I'd really just like to go home now."

"But it's your birthday," he reminded her. "And I'd really like to take you out to celebrate it."

She didn't feel like celebrating, but the thought of spending the few hours that were left of her birthday alone was too depressing to contemplate. And while the thought of spending those hours with Corey was tempting, she knew it would be dangerous to do so.

"Come on, Erin," he cajoled. "You didn't eat anything at the party. Let me at least buy you a burger."

"A burger?"

"Or steak and lobster—whatever you want."

She was too raw and vulnerable right now to resist him—and too pathetically needy to refuse. And she was kind of hungry. "I think I'd like a burger."

He took her hand, linking their fingers together. "Just a burger—or are you going to go crazy and order a side of fries?"

"Maybe onion rings."

"A woman after my own heart," he teased, squeezing her hand.

Erin forced a smile as she let him lead her to his truck.

Maybe she did want his heart—but she no longer believed that he would ever give it to her.

Chapter Thirteen

They went to the Hitching Post. Being a Saturday night, they expected to have to wait for a table, but they lucked out by walking in just as another couple was getting up to leave.

Corey helped Erin with her coat, hanging it on the hook beside their booth.

"Is that a new dress?"

She glanced down, as if she wasn't sure what she was wearing, then shook her head. "The only thing I've bought new since I came to Montana are jeans, flannel shirts and boots."

He slid onto the bench across from her. "I guess a California girl's wardrobe is pretty short on those."

"If by 'short' you mean 'nonexistent,' then yes."

"Well, you sure know how to wear them," he told her. "Although I must admit, I really like the way this fluttery little skirt shows off your legs."

She glanced at him over the top of her menu. "Are you flirting with me?"

"Why do you sound so surprised?"

"The last time I saw you, you made it pretty clear that we were done."

Corey started to respond, then noticed the waitress approaching. They ordered their drinks and burgers with a side of onion rings. When their server had gone, he said, "I was caught off guard by Delores's visit and my response was probably both impulsive and unfair."

"Is that an apology?"

"I am sorry," he told her. "And I don't want to lose what we had."

"What did we have, Corey?"

"If you're trying to make me squirm by asking me to talk about our relationship, you're going to be disappointed, darlin'."

The waitress returned with their drinks. Erin picked up her glass of wine and took a sip.

"I came here for a burger, not a relationship analysis," she told him.

"I'm not sure how much longer my business is going to keep me in Thunder Canyon," he said.

"I never expected you would stay here forever." Her tone was casual, but she looked away, giving him hope that she wasn't as unaffected by his announcement as she wanted to seem.

"How about you?" he asked. "How long do you think you'll be in Montana?"

She shrugged. "Right now, I don't have any plans to be anywhere else."

"Ever thought of spending some time in Texas?" he asked.

"No," she said bluntly.

"You're determined to make this difficult, aren't you?"

"That's not my intention," she denied.

"Just a lucky coincidence?"

"*You* would think it was a coincidence."

He winced. "Okay—I deserved that."

She sighed. "No, you didn't. I'm just not very good company tonight."

"Turning twenty-six is getting you down?"

Her lips curved, just a little. "That must be it."

He reached across the table, touched her hand. "Are you missing your family?"

"I guess I am. Which is silly because they're coming for Thanksgiving, but I've never been away on my birthday before."

"Tell me some of your favorite birthday memories," he suggested.

"Why?"

"Because it might help you feel less homesick."

"I'm not homesick," she denied automatically. Then, when his brows rose, she relented, "Not really."

"Would you have gone out for dinner if you were celebrating your birthday in San Diego?"

She shook her head. "My mother would have cooked— anything I wanted. And she would have made her famous triple-layer dark-chocolate coconut cake."

"Instead you're getting a hamburger."

Erin smiled as the waitress set her plate in front of her. "Yeah, but it's a really good burger. And onion rings," she said, plucking one from her plate and biting into it.

They didn't talk much while they ate, but the silence wasn't at all uncomfortable. Corey wasn't entirely sure that Erin had forgiven him for his dismissal of her baby-switch theory, but she seemed to be warming up to him, at least a little.

He excused himself when he'd finished his burger but detoured on his way to the men's room to track down their server and arrange for dessert. When their plates had been cleared away and Erin was finishing her second glass of wine, the waitress brought a chocolate fudge brownie with coconut sprinkled on top and a single candle stuck in the middle.

Erin's eyes widened.

"I'm sure this can't compare to anything your mother would have made, but it was the best I could do on short notice."

"You didn't have to do anything," she told him.

He nodded toward the dessert. "Make a wish and blow out your candle."

She focused on the candle, closed her eyes and blew softly. The flame flickered, then disappeared in a wisp of smoke.

She cut the brownie in half and insisted on sharing it with him. He didn't really like coconut, but since it was the first overture she'd made in his direction, he accepted happily.

When the plate was empty and the bill had been paid, he helped her into her coat again.

"Thank you," Erin said as she walked beside him toward the exit.

"For what?"

"For the rescue, for dinner and for hanging with me so that I didn't have to spend my birthday alone."

"Anytime," he told her.

She puzzled over his response.

A few days earlier, Corey had refused to consider the possibility that there had been a mix-up at the hospital. Of course, a few days earlier, Erin hadn't known about Elise's birthmark and proving that Jake and Josh had the same mark might have helped Corey see things from her point of view. But she hadn't shown him the photos of her brothers until after they'd left the party, after he'd unexpectedly come to her rescue.

So what had caused his change of heart? Did he really want to pick up their relationship where they'd let off? Why was he suddenly willing to forgive her deception?

She had no idea how to answer those questions and too many other things to worry about right now. Top of the list of her worries was how to tell her parents—Jack and Betty—what had happened at the hospital on the day that she was born. Thankfully, she had a few days to come up with the right words.

She was quiet on the drive back to her condo, thinking about their upcoming visit. And maybe it was because they were on her mind that she didn't find it strange when she saw their car in her driveway.

"You have company," Corey said.

His words made her realize that what she was seeing was real and not an illusion.

"My parents," she said.

"Did you know they were coming?"

She shook her head. "Not today."

Her hand was on the door handle even before he'd come to a complete stop, and then she was flying down the driveway and into her dad's arms.

"Dad." Tears filled her eyes as she moved from Jack's embrace to Betty's. "Mom. I thought you weren't coming until Wednesday."

"Well, that was the original plan," Jack admitted.

"But your birthday is today," Betty pointed out. "And there was no way I was missing my little girl's birthday if I didn't have to."

"What time did you get here? Why didn't you call me and let me know you were coming?"

"We wanted it to be a surprise."

"Well, it is," Erin said and hugged her again. "A wonderful surprise."

"Then you don't mind that we didn't get you a present?" Jack teased.

"Just having you here is the best present ever," she assured them.

"You're sure it's okay that we came a few days early?" Betty asked, glancing pointedly at Corey.

"Of course it is," Erin said, but she felt her cheeks flush as she imagined what they were thinking and how to introduce the man who had been her lover and now…was not. "This is Corey."

He shook hands with each of her parents, who didn't even try to be subtle as they sized him up. Her father's narrow-eyed gaze warned her that he was reserving judgment; her mother's warm smile suggested a willingness to be accepting. Of course, her mother had been willing to accept Trevor, too, and now that Erin was twenty-six years old (officially "over-the-hill" to a woman who had married when she was barely twenty), her matchmaking efforts would undoubtedly kick into overdrive.

"Are you going to make your parents stand in the driveway all night?" Corey asked her.

"Of course not," Erin denied. "Although as I stand here, I am wondering if I left my breakfast dishes on the counter this morning."

"I won't be surprised if you did," Betty said.

"And I don't care if you did," Jack said. "I'm just hoping you've got a cold beer in your fridge."

"I'm sure we can find one," Erin said, digging in her purse for her keys.

"I'll say goodbye then," Corey said to her, "so that you can have some time alone with your parents to catch up."

Erin was relieved by his offer. She didn't want her mother making more of her relationship with Corey than it was—especially when she had no idea what exactly it was right now.

"Thanks again for dinner," she said.

"You don't have to run off on our account," Jack said, obviously wanting more time to make up his mind about the man who'd been out with his daughter.

"And you can't go until you've had cake," Erin's mom insisted, reaching into the backseat for a covered plate.

"Triple-layer dark-chocolate coconut?" Corey asked.

Betty positively beamed. "Erin told you?"

"She said it didn't feel like her birthday without it."

"Then you really have to try a piece," she insisted.

So Corey came in and had a piece of cake and a cup of coffee.

Erin had thought it would be awkward to have him there, but her thoughts were so preoccupied that she was grateful for his efforts to keep the conversation flowing. While he was chatting with her father, she went upstairs to put sheets on the bed in the spare room. She was just pulling up the comforter when her mom came in.

"Your young man is helping Jack with the bags," Betty told her.

And so it begins, Erin thought, but with more indulgence than annoyance. "He's not my young man," she warned.

Not unexpectedly, her mother sighed. "Only because you're not trying hard enough, I'm sure."

She had to smile. It was either that or take her mother by the shoulders and shake her. But she couldn't deny that Betty had her best interests at heart—they just didn't always agree on what was "best" for Erin.

Thankfully, the arrival of Corey and her dad with the suitcases saved her from having to answer. While her parents got ready for bed, she saw Corey to the door.

"Should I apologize?" she asked him.

"For what?"

"Whatever my father may have said to you outside."

He grinned. "No need. In fact, I think we came to something of an understanding."

"What kind of understanding?"

"I understand that if I make a move on his daughter while he's sleeping under her roof, he's going to kick my ass."

"He's always been a little overprotective."

"You're his little girl," Corey said simply.

But was she? The automatic question brought tears to her eyes.

Corey tipped her chin up. "You are," he said, somehow reading the doubts that were in her mind. "And I suspect that you always will be, no matter how many birthdays you celebrate and no matter what a DNA test might prove."

She nodded.

"I'm glad I got to meet them," he told her.

"If I don't have to apologize for my dad, I should at least warn you about my mom."

"Why?"

"Because you made a very favorable impression on her and, if you're not careful, she'll have me out shopping for china patterns before the end of the week."

"Maybe I don't want to be careful," he said.

"Corey—"

"I know. I've done a complete one-eighty and you're trying to figure out why."

She eyed him warily.

"I'm not sure there's a simple explanation. As a result of my own history, I can handle almost anything but dishonesty. And when I thought you'd lied to me, well, I may have overreacted," he admitted. "But after I'd had some time to think about it, I realized that even if you had promised not to pursue the truth about the circumstances of your birth, I had no right to ask you to make such a promise."

"I needed to know," she said, needing *him* to understand how important that knowledge was to her.

He nodded. "And maybe you had a point when you said that I couldn't know how you felt because I'd never had reason to question where I fit in my family."

"Are you saying that you understand now?"

"I'm trying," he promised her. "But mostly, I'm saying that our relationship is worth the effort and if we have differences of opinion, we should work through them."

"You were the one who gave me the ultimatum," she reminded him.

"I was wrong."

"And if I told you I was taking out a billboard to announce that I'm Helen Clifton's daughter?"

"I'd try to talk you out of it," he said. "But only because I think the situation should be handled a little more discreetly."

She must have frowned, because he rubbed his thumb over her brow. "You're tired and you've had a long day. Don't stress about it now, darlin'."

"How can I not?"

"Try to think of something else," he said, and touched his lips to hers.

It was a fleeting kiss—filled with more promise than passion. She only wished she knew what he was promising.

Erin woke up the next morning to the mouthwatering scents of frying bacon and perking coffee. She slipped out of bed and into her robe and followed her nose downstairs to the kitchen.

"I didn't think I had any bacon," she said, pouring herself a cup of coffee from the pot.

"You didn't," Betty agreed. "You never have much more than the bare essentials, so I brought a few things in a cooler."

Erin opened the refrigerator to get the milk to add to her coffee and immediately realized that her mother had brought more than a few things—her fridge had never been so thoroughly stocked.

"Even out here in the wilds of Montana, there are grocery stores," she told her mom.

Betty stacked a couple of slices of French toast on a plate, added a few slices of bacon, then passed the plate to her daughter. "Sit and eat."

Erin sat and ate.

Usually breakfast was a bowl of cereal or some fruit and yogurt. She couldn't remember the last time she'd had French toast. And as much as she loved bacon—she took another bite of the deliciously salty meat—she never took the time to cook it for herself.

She picked up the bottle of maple syrup, poured some more onto her plate and swirled a piece of toast in it. "There are probably a gazillion calories in this breakfast."

"Calories don't count when food is prepared with love," Betty said.

"You always say that," Erin noted, dropping her gaze to her plate again so her mom wouldn't see the tears in her eyes.

"And you look like you could use a good meal—honestly, Erin, you're little more than skin and bones now."

She smiled at that because she knew it was far from the truth. She weighed exactly the same as always, but if Betty wasn't personally feeding her daughter, she had a tendency to assume that Erin wasn't eating.

"Where's Dad?" she asked, as much to shift the conversation as because she wanted to know.

"He had his breakfast already and went out for a walk— he was curious to check out the resort property." Betty carried her own mug of coffee to the table. "If you had to leave San Diego for a while, you couldn't have picked a prettier spot."

The front door opened and heavy footsteps pounded on the mat. "Brr, I think I've got ice on my glasses," Jack called out.

Erin smiled. "It is a little colder here than in California, though."

"A little?" Betty wrapped her cardigan more closely around herself.

"There's my girls," Jack said, coming into the kitchen. He pressed his cold cheek to his daughter's, then to his wife's.

Betty yelped. "Goodness, Jack. You're freezing."

"The air is brisk out there," he said. "But it sure does get the blood flowing."

Erin pushed her now-empty plate aside, smiling as she watched her dad make his way around her kitchen, finding the mug he'd obviously used earlier and refilling it with fresh coffee.

She'd missed these casual morning conversations with her parents, but she had different routines now—daily rituals that were her own. And maybe that was all part of growing up. Before she'd come to Thunder Canyon, she'd only occasionally thought about moving out of their home. Sure, she'd realized that she would have to make her own way eventually, but she'd had no real complaints about living under their roof, and the advantages had certainly outweighed the disadvantages.

But now that she had been living on her own for several months, she understood that it was what she'd needed—to be completely independent, to be responsible for herself, to make her own decisions. There was one decision in particular that she'd wrestled with late into the night—when to tell them what she'd learned about the events surrounding her birth at Thunder Canyon General Hospital. And she knew that she couldn't delay any longer.

"Mom. Dad." She took a deep breath, looked at each of them in turn and sent up a silent but fervent prayer that she was doing the right thing. "There's something I have to tell you."

Chapter Fourteen

"Do you remember last June, when I went to visit Aunt Erma?" Erin asked them.

"She had asked to see you," Jack recalled.

"It was just before she passed away," Betty added.

Erin nodded. "Well, she wanted to talk to me because she had some information that led her to believe that I had family in Thunder Canyon."

Betty looked to Jack, as if he might know something she didn't.

He shook his head. "If Erma had any relatives here, I didn't know about it."

"She didn't mean that she had family here, but that *I* did," Erin clarified.

"I don't understand," her mother said.

"I didn't understand either," Erin admitted. "She gave me some bits and pieces of information, but I never got a chance to ask her to explain."

She was making a mess of this, trying to break the news gently rather than blurting out 'I'm not your daughter.' But even if she could have spoken those words, she realized they weren't true. Corey was right—even if Betty Castro had not given birth to her, she would always be her mother.

"Is that why you came to Thunder Canyon?"

"Partly," Erin said, then realized her response was yet another half-truth and that she needed to be completely honest. "No, I left San Diego partly for the reasons I told you—because I was feeling stifled at the hotel and with Trevor. But I chose Thunder Canyon because of the questions I had."

"Because of Erma," Betty said, annoyance in her tone.

Jack laid his hand over his wife's. "What kind of questions?" he asked.

So Erin summarized, as best she could, her final conversation with her father's aunt and the information she'd uncovered since coming to Thunder Canyon, including the sense of recognition she'd felt when she saw the photo of Grant's sister at Erika and Dillon's wedding and the revelations from her recent conversation with Delores Beckett.

Her parents listened, silently absorbing what she was telling them, but she could tell that they were both confused and distressed by the implications.

"It seems…unbelievable," Jack said.

"Because it is," Betty insisted. "And I refuse to give any credence to Erma's crazy rants or to…"

Her words trailed off when Erin slid her digital camera across the table.

On the display was a picture of Elise that she'd snapped just before leaving her party the night before. She was with Grant, laughing at something he'd said, and the angle of the shot clearly showed the birthmark on the side of her nose.

Obviously Betty noticed it, too, because her breath caught. "Who is this?"

"Her name is Elise Clifton. She was born in Thunder Canyon General Hospital on November twentieth, twenty-six years ago."

Jack touched his wife's hand again.

"Helen Clifton's little girl." Her mother's words confirmed that she also remembered the woman she'd met in the maternity ward that day so many years earlier. "I didn't think it was possible—I didn't want to believe it was possible. But, oh, my Lord, the birthmark, and the shape of her eyes is exactly like Jake's, and the chin is so much like Josh's…"

She trailed off again and looked at Erin, who smiled wryly. "I know. She looks a lot more like my brothers than I do."

"But that might just be a coincidence," Betty said now, though not very convincingly.

"And I might believe it was," Erin said, "if not for all of the other coincidences."

Betty sighed, her eyes filled with tears. "Oh, honey. I don't know what to say."

While his wife and daughter fumbled, it was Jack who found the words. "I think the most important thing to remember at this point," he said to Erin, "is that we love you. We always have and we always will, and even if it turns out that a mistake was made and you aren't ours by blood, that will never change. You are our daughter in our hearts and that's more important than anything else."

It was probably the longest speech Erin had ever heard her father make, and though his tone was gruff, she knew that he meant every word. And because she finally understood that it was true, she fell into his arms and sobbed.

* * *

A while later, after all the tears had been dried, Betty asked, "What do you want to do now?"

"I want to tell Helen and Elise and Grant, Helen's son. But Corey told me that John's death hit them all hard, and I'm worried about how they'll react to finding out that their ties to one another aren't quite what they believed."

"You've talked to Corey about this?" Jack asked.

"I had to talk to someone," Erin told him.

"Then we'll talk about Corey later," her father promised.

"Why?"

"Because I know what it means when a man looks at a woman the way he was looking at my little girl, and I want to know what's going on with you two."

"Jack," Betty chided gently, as if she hadn't tried to pry the same information from Erin the night before. "She's a grown woman now."

"I said we'll talk about it later," he repeated.

And Erin smiled because she realized that although her entire life had been turned upside down, some things never changed.

"Getting back to the topic at hand," Betty said, looking pointedly at her husband before turning her attention back to her daughter. "I think you should talk to Helen first—a mom usually has a good idea about how her kids will deal with tough news."

"And my mom always has the best ideas," Erin said, making Betty smile. "If I could set up a meeting, would you go with me?"

"Absolutely," her mother said, proving once again that her support was unconditional and unwavering.

Corey was pulling into the Super Saver Mart parking lot, thinking about Erin instead of the groceries he needed, when he saw her walk out of the store. He recognized her Kia and pulled into a vacant spot beside it.

She looked up when he opened the door.

"Did Mother Hubbard find the cupboard was bare?" he asked lightly.

Her face was pale and her eyes looked tired, but she smiled, just a little. "I'd swear my mother brought half of the Whole Foods Market from San Diego in coolers," she told him. "But she somehow managed to forget butter."

"You don't have butter?" he asked curiously.

"No, I have margarine, and when my mother bakes, she does not substitute margarine for butter."

He stroked a finger gently over the shadow beneath her eye. "Rough night?"

"I didn't sleep well," she admitted.

"Probably because you were sleeping alone," he said teasingly, earning another half-smile from her.

"I told my parents this morning."

"How did they react?"

"They were shocked. Skeptical. But when they saw Elise's picture, they couldn't deny the possibility. We're going to talk to Helen before any other steps are taken."

"Sounds reasonable," he said.

She nodded.

"Speaking of next steps," he said. "How about catching a movie with me tonight?"

"My parents are visiting," she reminded him.

"They can come, too. Or are you worried that they won't approve of you dating me?"

"You know that's not the issue. And I'm not dating you."

"Don't shut me out, Erin."

"I'm not shutting you out," she denied. "I just need time to figure some things out."

"You don't have to figure everything out on your own," he told her. "Or are you saying 'no' to punish me for not supporting you?"

"I'm not punishing you."

He wasn't sure he believed her, but he also couldn't blame her. He'd treated her carelessly and she had every right to be wary. But he wasn't going to give up. He would do whatever he needed to do to prove his feelings for her, to prove that they were meant to be together because he really believed that they were.

"Okay," he finally said. "I'll give you some time to figure things out. But while you're doing that, there's one other piece of information you might want to consider."

"Which is?"

"That I'm in love with you."

Erin stared at him, stunned, breathless, terrified.

"Yeah, that's kind of how I felt when the realization hit me," Corey told her. "And I probably shouldn't have said those words for the first time in the middle of a parking lot, but I wanted you to know."

It wasn't the location but the words that left her speechless. They'd broken up; he'd walked out on her. "You don't—you can't mean it."

His brows rose. "Why can't I?"

She didn't know why, she only knew that he couldn't. It didn't make any sense. She looked away from him, trying to order her scrambled thoughts, and bought some time for herself by unlocking the doors and putting the butter inside her car.

He took her hands and linked their fingers together. "I know you're confused and probably more than a little scared because of your family situation. But although Helen may have given birth to you and genetics might make Grant your brother, Betty and Jack Castro are still your parents—they raised you and loved you and helped you become the woman you are now. The woman *I* love."

He sounded sincere and she wanted to believe that he meant what he said, but it wasn't that long ago that he'd dumped her. He'd walked away from her when she'd needed him and, in the process, he'd trampled all over her heart with his size thirteen boots. And now he thought he could toss those three little words out and she would welcome him back with open arms? Not likely.

But you love him, too.

The voice didn't echo in her head this time but in her heart, but she refused to listen.

"I can't do this right now," she told him.

"I'm not asking you to do or say anything," he told her. "I just wanted you to know because I'm going back to Texas—"

"You're leaving?" She didn't know why the thought sent her into such a panic. After all, she was the one who'd told him to go, but she'd only wanted him to give her a little space—not fifteen-hundred miles.

And now that she knew he was leaving Thunder Canyon, she suddenly wanted to cling to him and ask him to stay. Because she was afraid of being alone? Or because she was afraid that if he walked out the door he might never come back?

"Only for a while," he promised. "And I will be coming back."

When?

The question sprang to her lips, but this time she managed to bite back the instinctive response. She had no right to ask questions, no right to expect anything from him. And she should know better than to expect anything from a man who could say he loved her in one breath and tell her that he was leaving in the next.

It was for the best, she decided. Because she needed to figure out her own life before she could decide where he might fit into it—or even if she wanted him to.

"When are you leaving?" she asked instead.

"Tomorrow."

She nodded and tried to ignore the tightness that had taken hold of her chest.

"I'm giving you some time." He tipped her chin up and pressed a brief, hard kiss to her lips. "But I'm not going to wait forever for you to decide what you want."

He started across the parking lot.

"Corey."

He paused, turned.

She wasn't sure what she'd intended to say, what she could say, that would erase the aching emptiness that filled her heart as she watched him walk away from her. In the end, she only said, "Have a safe trip."

He nodded.

She watched until the automatic doors of the store had closed behind him, then she got into her car and drove home.

The Clifton and the Castro families spent Thanksgiving together. Bo and Holly Clifton were in attendance, and even Erin's brothers, Jake and Josh, made the trip to Thunder Canyon for the holiday. Erin knew their decision was partly motivated by a desire to reassure her that they would always be around to nag her, as big brothers are required to do, and partly motivated by curiosity about their new sister. Although they were still waiting for the DNA results to officially confirm that the babies had been incorrectly ID'd at the hospital, no one doubted that it was true. Betty shared the information that she had with Helen and was, in turn, given one final piece of the puzzle.

When Helen first held her baby girl in her arms, she hadn't had a birthmark on the side of her nose. A few hours later, after the baby had been bathed and swaddled and returned to her, she'd questioned the nurse about the tiny brown mark that she saw on her daughter's face and that she was certain hadn't been there before. The nurse had brushed off her question, assuring her that birthmarks weren't always present at birth and often did appear hours—or even days and weeks—later.

Because of the hemorrhaging, Betty hadn't seen her baby until after her surgery, so she couldn't say for sure that her daughter had been born with a birthmark, but she remembered that the marks had been evident on each of her sons right away.

Learning that she had a second mother and a father again, after losing John so many years earlier, seemed to have completely overwhelmed Elise.

Erin could understand—she'd felt the same way when she'd come to Thunder Canyon on the impetus of only her great-aunt Erma's cryptic words. And though her suspicions about her background had continued to grow over the past few months, hearing Delores Beckett give credence to those suspicions had made her question everything she knew about her roots and her family. Elise, having never had any reason to doubt who she was or where she came from, was still reeling from the revelations. Erin hoped that in time Elise would agree that they weren't losing the families they'd known but gaining new ones, with the added bonus that sharing brothers made them honorary sisters. But she understood that the other woman needed some time to absorb the revelations that had been thrown at her. As Corey had once pointed out to her, Erin had been thinking about the possibility of a baby mix-up for several weeks, and Elise had known the truth for only a few days.

As always, just thinking of Corey made her heart ache. She hadn't heard from him since he'd left Thunder Canyon, and through everything else that had happened, she'd remained conscious of his absence, of how empty her life seemed without him. True, she'd told him she needed time, but she thought he could at least have called.

Or you could've called him.

Damn, but there were times when she hated that rational side of her.

She knew it was her turn to make the next move. No way was she going to let her last memory of Corey Traub be of him walking across the parking lot of the Super Saver Mart.

Erin had to work the Friday and Saturday immediately following Thanksgiving, but her parents stayed through to Sunday morning and spent a lot of time with Elise and Helen. As she went about her usual routine, it surprised Erin how normal everything seemed. On the outside everything was exactly the same, but on the inside so much had changed—and definitely for the better.

Since the summer, she'd been living in limbo—trying to answer questions about her past and not at all certain about her future. Recent events had somehow solidified her relationship with her parents and her brothers, and she was building new ones with Helen and Elise and Grant and Stephanie. It was her new sister-in-law who pointed out to Erin that she was going to be an aunt very soon, and she knew that both she and Elise would spoil the baby terribly when he or she finally arrived.

She had so much to be grateful for—her life was full

and rich. And still, there was an emptiness inside of her, a space that she knew only Corey could fill.

I'm not going to wait forever for you to decide what you want.

His words echoed in the back of her mind.

Okay, seven days wasn't exactly forever, but it certainly felt like it.

When she went into work the next day, she was going to ask Grant for some time off, and if she had to play the sister card, well, she wasn't above doing so. She wasn't going to wait another seven days to book a plane ticket to Texas.

Just making the decision made her heart feel lighter, and she resolved to check the flight schedule to Texas so that she could discuss specific options when she talked to Grant. She was booting up her computer when the doorbell rang.

Erin peeked through the side window, but she didn't see anyone on her porch. All she could see was a huge evergreen tree, but she was pretty sure it hadn't pressed the bell.

She pulled open the door for a closer look. The tree topped six feet and was at least that wide at the bottom. And behind it—laden down with shopping bags—was Corey.

Her heart started pounding; her knees trembled. She wanted to throw her arms around him, but there was no way she could get near him with that forest between them, so instead she only asked, "When did you get back?"

"Can I come in and put this stuff down?" he asked.

She automatically stepped back. Somehow he maneuvered around the massive tree and through the doorway.

"Late last night," he answered her original question.

"What the heck is all of that?" she asked, indicating the bags in his arms.

"Decorations."

"Why?"

He nodded in the direction of the evergreen propped up on her porch. "Because the tree will look much more festive when it's dressed up."

"Okay, maybe the question I should have asked is, why did you bring me a Christmas tree?"

"Because Erika said you didn't have one yet."

She watched as he wrestled the tree through the doorway. It occurred to her that maybe she should offer to assist him, but she would probably be more of a hindrance than a help, so she just stayed out of his way.

When the tree was inside, he stepped into the family room and turned in a slow circle, surveying the location. "Between the window and the fireplace?"

She pushed the wing chair aside to make room.

He came over to help her—then pulled her into his arms. He felt so good—so solid and strong—that she melted against him. And for a moment, she just held on, breathing in the warm, masculine scent of him and marveling at the fact that he was there. He was really there.

"I guess I won't have to make that trip to Texas after all," she said.

"You were planning to go to Texas?"

"Well, I wasn't going to wait for you forever."

"Forever?" His brows rose. "I've been gone a week."

She slid her arms around his neck and pulled his head down to hers, kissing him softly. "It was a really long week."

"Tell me about it, darlin'," he said.

She shook her head. "I don't want to talk."

He caught her hands as they began to tug at his clothes. "I promised myself that I wasn't going to pressure you. I wanted to give you the time you said you needed, and it hasn't been that much time, but—"

"It was enough," she interrupted.

Ever since he'd walked away from her in the parking lot of the grocery store a week earlier, Corey had lived with an uncomfortable pressure in his chest. With Erin's words, her kiss, and her touch, the painful tightness finally eased.

She touched her mouth to his again. He let her set the pace, content to just hold her, so happy to have her in his arms again. But when she deepened the kiss, when her soft breasts flattened against his chest and her hips pressed against his, he felt the pressure building again, but it was much lower this time.

As passions escalated, clothes fell away, until they were both naked and panting and wanting.

"I should take you upstairs," he said.

But she shook her head. "I want you here—like our first time."

So he tugged the blanket off the back of the sofa and spread it out on the floor.

Her skin was pale, creamy silk that trembled when his hands stroked over her. He wrapped her hair around his hand, and tugged her head back, feasted on the long, slim column of her throat, savored the frantic pounding of her pulse. His lips moved lower until he found her breast, and he laved and suckled until she was whimpering and shuddering beneath him.

She reached down between their bodies, seeking and finding the hard length of him. And when her fingers wrapped around him, he knew that he was as close to the edge as she was.

"I want you inside me," she told him.

"I want to be inside you," he admitted.

Later he might regret that he hadn't taken more time with

her, that there had been no quiet words or soft caresses. But in the moment, the need was too great. They would have a lifetime to take things slow—at least if he had anything to say about it—but for now, her hands were as rough and frantic as his, her kisses equally greedy and demanding.

"Now," she said breathlessly.

Now, his body echoed her plea, and he sank into the sweet, wet haven between her thighs.

Her muscles clamped down on him, and he groaned at the pleasure of being so tightly and intimately embraced. Then he began to move, and her head fell back as she closed her eyes and surrendered to the delicious friction of their mating.

She'd missed him.

Not just the intimacy of their lovemaking, but simply being with Corey. And as Erin lay cradled in the warm strength of his arms, her body still joined with his, she knew that she had finally found where she wanted to be.

"I've figured out what I want," she said.

"What's that?" he asked, skimming his fingers down her back.

"I want you in my life. It doesn't matter whether I'm in San Diego or Thunder Canyon or Texas, so long as I'm with you."

"Well, lucky for me, that fits right into my plans."

"Which part?"

"The part where we're together."

"I love you," she said softly.

He brushed her hair away from her face, kissed her gently. "It seems as if I've waited forever to hear you say those words."

"Forever? You were only gone a week," she said, echoing his earlier statement.

"It was a really long week," he told her.

She pressed closer to him. "Tell me about it."

He rolled away from her, laughing. "We can't spend all day on this floor."

"Why not?"

"Because we've got a tree to decorate, darlin'."

It took them a while, but they finally did get the tree set up. Erin tried to help Corey with the lights, but the needles were sharp and after she'd hissed several times in response to being poked, he sent her into the kitchen to make hot chocolate.

By the time she returned with two steaming cups, the tree was illuminated from top to bottom with hundreds of tiny colored lights.

"What do you think?"

She thought it was perfect, but she wasn't going to tell him that. Instead, she looked it over carefully, critically. "There are more lights at the top than the bottom."

"I was running out." He came over to stand beside her, eyeing the tree up and down, then shrugged. "Well, next year you're doing the lights, no matter how much you whine."

Next year.

She liked the sound of that but felt compelled to protest, "I did not whine."

"You did so whine." He looked at her out of the corner of his eye, grinned. "And now you're pouting."

"I don't pout," she denied.

Corey took one of the mugs from her hand and sipped. "I dated a woman once—well, I've dated a few women," he said, as if telling her something she didn't know, "but this was one I was dating around the holidays—and she had this stunning Christmas tree. Every branch was full and precisely shaped, the decorations were beautiful and color coordinated. It was the most perfect tree I'd ever seen."

She wasn't sure where he was going with the story, but she couldn't resist cocking her head slightly to the side, so that the slightly off-balance tree would appear straight. "You mean like this one?"

He shrugged. "It may not be perfect, but it's real. Which is what I realized was wrong with my relationship with Rebecca—she was always so precisely put together, so perfect and unreal. And the longer I stood there, looking at the tree that was so much like Rebecca, the more I realized that I didn't want perfection."

"I'm not perfect," she warned him.

"Neither am I," he admitted, "but I think we're perfect for one another."

She smiled. "I can live with that."

"Can you live with me?" he asked.

Her heart skipped. "Are you asking me to?"

"Actually, I don't want to live with you—I want to marry you."

She'd barely had a chance to get her head around the idea of living with him and he'd moved straight into talk about marriage. "For a man who talks slow, you sure move fast."

"The usual response is a 'yes' or a 'no,'" he told her. "Preferably 'yes.'"

"If those are my only options, I'll go with 'yes.'"

"Really?"

"Do you want me to change my answer?"

"No way." He pulled her close and brushed his lips against hers. "I've got you now, darlin', and I'm never letting you go."

She settled into his embrace, not wanting him to ever

let go, not wanting to be anywhere but precisely where she was.

So much had changed in her life since that last meeting with her great aunt Erma, and though there were times when she'd questioned her decision to come to Thunder Canyon, she wouldn't wish any of it away because it had brought her here—to this time and place and this man.

She wondered what Erma would have thought of Corey, if she'd had a chance to meet him. No doubt her aunt would have loved him.

"What are you smiling about?" Corey asked her.

"Just thinking about how very lucky I am."

He kissed her again. "I'm glad you came home to Thunder Canyon."

"Me, too." She'd come to town in search of a family, but she'd found so much more.

She snuggled deeper into his arms, secure in the knowledge that she was where she truly belonged.

* * * * *

Don't miss A THUNDER CANYON CHRISTMAS
by RaeAnne Thayne
The next book in
MONTANA MAVERICKS:
THUNDER CANYON COWBOYS
On sale December 2010,
wherever Silhouette books are sold.

COMING NEXT MONTH
Available November 30, 2010

#2083 A THUNDER CANYON CHRISTMAS
RaeAnne Thayne
Montana Mavericks: Thunder Canyon Cowboys

#2084 UNWRAPPING THE PLAYBOY
Marie Ferrarella
Matchmaking Mamas

#2085 THE BACHELOR'S CHRISTMAS BRIDE
Victoria Pade
Northbridge Nuptials

#2086 ONCE UPON A CHRISTMAS EVE
Christine Flynn
The Hunt for Cinderella

#2087 TWINS UNDER HIS TREE
Karen Rose Smith
The Baby Experts

#2088 THE CHRISTMAS PROPOSITION
Cindy Kirk
Rx for Love

SPECIAL EDITION

REQUEST YOUR FREE BOOKS!

2 FREE NOVELS PLUS 2 FREE GIFTS!

SPECIAL EDITION
Life, Love and Family!

YES! Please send me 2 FREE Silhouette® Special Edition® novels and my 2 FREE gifts (gifts are worth about $10). After receiving them, if I don't wish to receive any more books, I can return the shipping statement marked "cancel." If I don't cancel, I will receive 6 brand-new novels every month and be billed just $4.24 per book in the U.S. or $4.99 per book in Canada. That's a saving of 15% off the cover price! It's quite a bargain! Shipping and handling is just 50¢ per book.* I understand that accepting the 2 free books and gifts places me under no obligation to buy anything. I can always return a shipment and cancel at any time. Even if I never buy another book from Silhouette, the two free books and gifts are mine to keep forever.

235/335 SDN E5RG

Name   (PLEASE PRINT)

Address   Apt. #

City   State/Prov.   Zip/Postal Code

Signature (if under 18, a parent or guardian must sign)

Mail to the Silhouette Reader Service:
IN U.S.A.: P.O. Box 1867, Buffalo, NY 14240-1867
IN CANADA: P.O. Box 609, Fort Erie, Ontario L2A 5X3

Not valid for current subscribers to Silhouette Special Edition books.

Want to try two free books from another line?
Call 1-800-873-8635 or visit www.morefreebooks.com.

* Terms and prices subject to change without notice. Prices do not include applicable taxes. N.Y. residents add applicable sales tax. Canadian residents will be charged applicable provincial taxes and GST. Offer not valid in Quebec. This offer is limited to one order per household. All orders subject to approval. Credit or debit balances in a customer's account(s) may be offset by any other outstanding balance owed by or to the customer. Please allow 4 to 6 weeks for delivery. Offer available while quantities last.

Your Privacy: Silhouette is committed to protecting your privacy. Our Privacy Policy is available online at www.eHarlequin.com or upon request from the Reader Service. From time to time we make our lists of customers available to reputable third parties who may have a product or service of interest to you. If you would prefer we not share your name and address, please check here. ☐

Help us get it right—We strive for accurate, respectful and relevant communications. To clarify or modify your communication preferences, visit us at www.ReaderService.com/consumerschoice.

SSE10R

*See below for a sneak peek from our classic
Harlequin® Romance® line.*

Introducing DADDY BY CHRISTMAS by Patricia Thayer.

Mɪᴀ caught sight of Jarrett when he walked into the open lobby. It was hard not to notice the man. In a charcoal business suit with a crisp white shirt and striped tie covered by a dark trench coat, he looked more Wall Street than small-town Colorado.

Mia couldn't blame him for keeping his distance. He was probably tired of taking care of her.

Besides, why would a man like Jarrett McKane be interested in her? Why would he want to take on a woman expecting a baby? Yet he'd done so many things for her. He'd been there when she'd needed him most. How could she not care about a man like that?

Heart pounding in her ears, she walked up behind him. Jarrett turned to face her. "Did you get enough sleep last night?"

"Yes, thanks to you," she said, wondering if he'd thought about their kiss. Her gaze went to his mouth, then she quickly glanced away. "And thank you for not bringing up my meltdown."

Jarrett couldn't stop looking at Mia. Blue was definitely her color, bringing out the richness of her eyes.

"What meltdown?" he said, trying hard to focus on what she was saying. "You were just exhausted from lack of sleep and worried about your baby."

He couldn't help remembering how, during the night, he'd kept going in to watch her sleep. How strange was that? "I hope you got enough rest."

She nodded. "Plenty. And you're a good neighbor for

coming to my rescue."

He tensed. Neighbor? *What neighbor kisses you like I did?* "That's me, just the full-service landlord," he said, trying to keep the sarcasm out of his voice. He started to leave, but she put her hand on his arm.

"Jarrett, what I meant was you went beyond helping me." Her eyes searched his face. "I've asked far too much of you."

"Did you hear me complain?"

She shook her head. "You should. I feel like I've taken advantage."

"Like I said, I haven't minded."

"And I'm grateful for everything…"

Grasping her hand on his arm, Jarrett leaned forward. The memory of last night's kiss had him aching for another. "I didn't do it for your gratitude, Mia."

Gorgeous tycoon Jarrett McKane has never believed in Christmas—but he can't help being drawn to soon-to-be-mom Mia Saunders! Christmases past were spent alone…and now Jarrett may just have a fairy-tale ending for all his Christmases future!

*Available December 2010,
only from Harlequin® Romance®.*

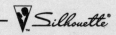

SPECIAL EDITION

USA TODAY BESTSELLING AUTHOR

MARIE FERRARELLA

BRINGS YOU ANOTHER
HEARTWARMING STORY FROM

When Lilli McCall disappeared on him
after he proposed, Kullen Manetti swore
never to fall in love again. Eight years later
Lilli is back in his life, threatening to break
down all the walls he's put up to
safeguard his heart.

UNWRAPPING
THE PLAYBOY

*Available December
wherever books are sold.*